Cyrus

JHN EXCLUSIVE

"For the love of Elizabeth Wilson."

Written By: Jacob L. Hollingsworth

JACOB HOLLINGSWORTH NETWORK CORPORATION

STORY

A young millionaire, Cyrus O'Brian, is set apart from any other finance middle-man in Double-City. He possesses the ability to control time with just the breath of his words. He has it all, except for the love of his life, Elizabeth Wilson, wrapped in his arms forever. To win her heart, Cyrus will travel to the past to right the one wrong of her life. Little did he know, he would be introduced to the despair of righting his own.

CYRUS – KEY

{} - NARRATION

[ ] - SCENE CHANGE

( ) - CHARACTER THOUGHT

* * - ACTION

JACOB HOLLINGSWORTH NETWORK CORPORATION

CYRUS S1C1: CYRUS

CYRUS: (Hello, my name is Cyrus O'Brian, and this...
is my city. 'Double-City', from end to end, I own it. I'm
your... "local" middleman, which means I make all the
deals: from bank transfers, stock exchanges, real-es-
tate lotteries, contract negotiations... I do it all. My corporation has reached one hundred thirty-five million
dollars that way. So yeah, that's a ton of money. My
net worth being ninety-five million because I hire a few
other guys to do my bidding; you know, when I'm out
of town working on vacation at Miami Beach. So a few
of my assets are working but I still own them so that
means it's calculated into my net worth of... ninety-five
million.)

*{Cyrus continues his walk up from his front gate
driveway on the left-hand side of his largely up-scaled
tower. It reads "CYRUS".}*

CYRUS: This is my office.

*{Cyrus makes his grand entrance into the white lobby
where he is greeted.}*

SECRETARY: Hello, Cyrus. You're late for your meeting again.

CYRUS: Hello, Rhonda—how's it going this fine evening?

RHONDA: It's going fine, but it's only 12:36 in the afternoon.

CYRUS: Details, Rhonda Scott... Only details that are quite relevant are necessary. Doesn't matter the time of day, if the money's still flowin'.

{*Cyrus walks through the lobby hands engraved in his trousers' pockets with people around him wearing tranquil slacks. He hops on the elevator at the end of the sanction up to the mid-floor where the company's meetings are usually held in conference rooms. Sleek, describing the area. Dark brown round tables in each room the size of an intern's entire work area. One room with a half-poured amount of slacks growing irritable of their current waiting situation. The elevator door "bings" at the floor of the conference rooms where Cyrus exits. He walks into the meeting room where the faces have now grown irritable at the site of Cyrus and his confidence in being so late to his own meeting. He makes his way to the head seat of the room and sits crossing his legs as if he were not in the wrong. And then he speaks one word.*}

CYRUS: **REWIND**.

The conference members remake their previous steps out of the office, and then back into the office.

{*All of the attendees walk into the room as they had before. Completely unaware that they had already previously performed these actions.*}

CYRUS: Hello, welcome! (I can control time.)

{*Later in the evening, Cyrus steps out into the night for a city-wide event called the 'St. John's National Foster Home Liberation'. A touring event that brought out America's most wealthy, and appeared in DoubleCity every year. There, he hops out of his grey slimmed sports car to valet. Then he tugs at his blazer jacket with both hands—not to make sure it fit appropriately, but to make sure he looked "okay" for the paparazzi cameras.*}

CYRUS: (After a full-on slate of boring negotiations like today, I like to go out and unwind. You know, like most millionaires with a taste for a very expensive lifestyle.)

{*Bustled around the gold and silver lighted runway to the entrance, the people with phones and cameras are trying to get the best angle on the most spectacular beings in town. Cyrus's golden hair sparkled as he walked upon the sidewalk.*}

PAPARAZZI GUY: Hey, Cyrus, would you mind pict'—would you mind taking a picture with me... for my sister? She's sick in the hospital. Her name's... her name's "Missy".

{*Cyrus examines the kid. Well put together. Hair slimmed back and blonde. The kid had a perfect smile as if he'd recently had his braces removed. Cyrus could also tell his suit had recently been pressed and rented, and also sized for him perfectly. With almost no signs of worry or stress that conceived the notion of "sick family member". Only the physical display of sleep depravity under his eyes.*}

CYRUS: ... I think you're lying.

PAPARAZZI GUY: I'm sorry?

{*Cyrus places a hand on his shoulder with a grim smile along his tilted face.*}

CYRUS: Your need for detail is too intact, kid. Better luck next time, right?

{*Cyrus walks inside the event leaving the young Paparazzi Guy baffled.*}

PAPARAZZI GUY #2: Yo', Jack! He didn't go for your B.S sob story?

{Cyrus walks in the silver-dazzled room where the lights shined from the ceiling upon the huge crowd of smiling faces. He crosses the center of the floor where he spots a brown-haired, emerald eyed beauty, and their eyes locked as if a sense of love had once been attained. Their glares sparkle widely, as the woman takes a gasp for air. Then Cyrus breaks the connection. With his hands still pressed and engraved in his pockets, he heads over to the bar East of the center of the room. The music in the place breathed a smooth breeze with live mezzo piano trumpets, drums, but the keyboard showed a for certain direction. As Cyrus crosses down the lobbying stairway onto the main floor, he spots a familiar lovely face. A medium shade brunette hair, blue eyes, about 5'7" inches tall. She could have been shorter, but Cyrus knew she was always around that size description. Wearing some purple dress—a male can never make out an appropriate description. With a beautiful smile that could light up the night the way fireflies do down south. Cyrus would always visit his cousins down south when he was a child, and the fireflies would always light up the night down there. Cyrus bent over at the bar east of the main floor where everyone chattered and bustled awaiting service. A brown-haired young male at the age of Cyrus bent over his left elbow on the bar to impose himself upon Cyrus.}

RANDOM GUY #1: Man, did you see her?

CYRUS: ... Yes, Curtis, I did.

CURTIS: Man, if I could get a girl like that, I would...

CYRUS: **PAUSE!**

Time stops

CYRUS: This is my best friend Curtis Loans. I've known him since I was a rowdy teenager, running on sex and drugs. Well, I still run on those things, but. . . you get the idea. Hey, I'm still young as fuck! Who gives a shit!? PLAY!

Time plays

CURTIS LOANS: ... marry her in no time. You need to propose.

CYRUS: What?

CURTIS LOANS: Just kidding. But you should go talk to her more often.

CYRUS: Curtis, we... aren't at that place yet; now would you relax! Geez.

CURTIS LOANS: Just sayin'. You guys have been out a few times and obviously you have feelings... you're just scared to commit to anything.

CYRUS: Yeah. Well, how about I commit to kicking your ass?

CURTIS LOANS Alright, alright. I'm just sayin': Just do it, man.

CYRUS: Alright, man—shit...

{*Cyrus spins in his silver-plated bar stool, pretends to check himself for fashion etiquette even though he knew that there was no need for it.*}

CYRUS: I'm good? Yeah, I'm good.

{*Cyrus gets up, and crosses the room where she stood. He approaches the one with the melon welcoming.*}

CYRUS: Hello, Elizabeth, I was just wondering if you would... you know, like to go out with me some time later next week, and then later... we could get married and have children, and... wow, that came out really, really bad. **REWIND!** ***Time rewinds***

CYRUS: Hey, Elizabeth, would you like to... ahh, **REWIND!**

Time rewinds

CYRUS: Elizabeth, I lov—... whoa, way too strong again... **REWIND!**

Time rewinds

CYRUS: Okay, come on, man you've done this like plenty times in your head and dreams. You've already been out with her before. Just do it again like you did the last time! Oh—but last time... (She didn't look so darn cute with that dress on. Just jeans, and a casual shirt with little cleavage and ruffles along the edges.)

{*Cyrus approaches her once more. And then, after numerous failed attempts, he finally got it "right"? Small talk has no room in a place like this. Best to get straight to your topic of conversation.*}

CYRUS: Hi, Elizabeth, would you like to... maybe have a drink with me sometime next week. I know you're busy and all but... I would really love your company? (Okay that was really good.)

ELIZABETH: Cyrus! How's it goin'!? Uhm, sure... are you free next week around. . . I don't know, Wednesday-ish?

CYRUS: Well actually, I believe I am. And if I weren't, I'd simply make time for you.

{Cyrus could see her cheeks flush red.}

ELIZABETH: Oh, okay then, Cy'. Then it's a date!

{Cyrus turns back with a stale grin and walks back over to the bar back to Curtis with a newfound glory.}

CURTIS: What'd she say?

CYRUS: What do you think?

CURTIS: "Get away from me?" AHAHAHA!

{Cyrus flashes an overconfident grin with low eyes. Curtis continues in laughter.}

CURTIS: Oh frick!

{*Both smile at each other and continue conversation. Meanwhile, there is a new set of lustful things sitting west of the bar. Maybe two, maybe three, maybe four. Cyrus lost count after his fourth drink. But he knew one was a redhead. All the girls make their way over to Cyrus. Placing hands and such things. Cyrus continues to reject the feelings of the moment. One of the girls then whispers naughty agendas into his left ear. Cyrus, blacking out, but Curtis is there and would make sure he would not regret the actions after such advancement with Elizabeth that night. Cyrus heads up to the front entrance with Curtis, and the groupies follow along. Cyrus stumbles upon a thought.*}

CYRUS: (I wonder if Liz' sees these groupies following me out. I do not remember giving them consent.)

{*But Elizabeth indeed sees the crowd leave the event rather early. They stagger with jitters into Cyrus's moonlit mobile. The night still dark as an abyss but still young in some minds. They arrive at Cyrus's condominium and head up to his place. The party continues for an hour or two. Drugs all over the sitting room table. The party rarely dies down before Curtis Loans clears the space of people, and even tries to straighten up a bit before helping up the rarely conscious Cyrus to his bedroom and onto the bed before prompting his due exit.*}

CYRUS S1C2:
FRANKENSTEIN IN
DOUBLE-CITY

TEENAGE KID#1: Cy'? CY!? You ready?

{A Young Cyrus abruptly nods with a seeming confidence.}

TEENAGE KID#1: Good. Sean, you ready, right?

SEAN: Yeah, I'm ready.

TEENAGE KID#1: Good.

{The three wait outside of a local drug store just south of their own county. It's 8:02 pm in the late Fall season. No one can spot them in the old mobile across the street, and south across that street from the store. The owner of the shop is closing up. He appears to be in his early fifties. Wearing a white t-shirt, and an apron. An Italian male with hairy arms. His name should be "Pigiono" as it says above the entrance in blue and red fainted, painted lettering. The paint looks old,

but not old enough that the man's name shouldn't be "Pigiono". The winds are heavy at this hour. While tatters of rain, as cold as the winter itself, drain and hit at a spacey pace. "Pigiono" seems to just be going through his usual closing routine.}

TEENAGE KID#1: Alright, let's go.

{Each of the three quickly hop out of the car simultaneously, all wearing hoods, except Cyrus. He knew he would not be spotted outside so he waits to slip on his black ski mask until he approaches the front curb of the general store. The three bolt through the front door as the bell above it sounds. The owner is indeed an Italian man; as the three get closer, you can now see the stubble of black and gray hairs around the brim of his face. Thinning, slick black hairs platted on the top of his head with a design in the back still set at your basic three-level clipper shave.}

ITALIAN MAN: What the hell!?

TEEN CYRUS: Don't make this difficult, old man!

TEENAGE KID#1: Don't make this difficult! Give up the money!

ITALIAN MAN: I'm not giving up shit!

{The Kid abruptly pulls up a firearm. A dull colored one. Gray. No look of concern on his body language as his hoodie covers his emotion. Rather an appearance of eagerness. Young Cyrus looks on with jitters and anticipation, wide-eyed. While Sean is hanging left behind The Kid. So quiet that if the situation got out of hand, Sean would still be there quiet.}

ITALIAN MAN: ... You stupid sonsa'-bitches. You think you can rob me!? Do you know who I am!? Well, do ya'!?

{The Kid still steady, Cyrus is a little shook, but also steady. So is Sean.}

TEEN CYRUS: ... We don't want anymore problems just... give us the money.

{The Kid with the gun still steady. The Italian Man takes a glare at Cyrus. He hears his words, but they do not reign much weight. He's angry, and he could sense the lack of certainty in Cyrus's voice angling at lack of experience. So angry, that you cannot see the anger on the exterior, but see it fuming within.}

ITALIAN MAN: You don't know who I am.

{The man starts to giggle.}

ITALIAN MAN: My people are gonna have your bastard heads hanging on the wall of my shop when I'm through with you—

TEENAGE KID: JUST HAND OVER THE DAMN MONEY! NOW! NOW! Or I swear I'll blow your fucking head off! —

TEEN CYRUS: Lance, relax.

SEAN: Lance!

{Sean finally breaks silence. Young Cyrus looks over at Sean and feels a sense of comfort that he's not the only one that believes Lance has taken this all too far! But it wouldn't matter if Sean agreed because Cyrus knew this had gone too far in his own imagination. Along with a feeling of heat and uneasiness under his ski mask and heavy grey jacket. Though he should feel like ice with the weather quivering outside.}

TEEN CYRUS: Lance.

LANCE: Shut up, Cyrus.

TEEN CYRUS: Lance put the damn gun down!

PIGIONO: Listen to your boy, kid! You think you're tough!? My boys are gonna have your family hanging up by their heads when we're done with you!

LANCE: Sean, go take the money. Bust it up if you have ta'.

{Sean obliges to Lance's wishes. Maybe he's so startled by the gun; he's under the control of fear from the weapon. He reaches over the shop's counter that's covered with packaged gum and cigarette lighters. Luckily, the register hadn't been locked. No harm to be done to the cash register. Sean just pulls it open and takes all the cash he could. It seems to be a decent amount. Sean crosses back over the shop quickly to side with his friends. It didn't take much time. The shop is no bigger than the size of a neighborhood laundromat.}

ITALIAN MAN: Son of a bitch, you not takin'—

POW!

{Young Cyrus saw it coming. He had realized Lance was out of control on a power trip the moment he drew that gun. Young Cyrus looked on with a forlorn confusion as the man fell in slow motion. Questions and replies rushed to the tip of his brain hanging outward like fresh stitches.}

TEEN CYRUS: (Lance? A criminal? My best friend? A killer? No way. Lance had only made a mistake; he is no sadistic killer. Sure he's had some mistakes in the past... like, when he stole that gum and those pencils from the teacher's desk. Or when he beat kids too much for picking on me. He even made fun of Curtis! But Curtis was judging me! He said I was hanging out with the wrong crowds too much. But Lance was the coolest 10th Grader in town, and he helped my dad work on his car last summer before we visited my Uncle Thomas down south. My Dad wasn't that handy. But Lance was. Curtis said I changed. But those were all genuine mistakes! But none this grave. So, this had to have been a mistake!)

LANCE: We gotta go.

{Cyrus wastes no more time pondering Lance's "mistakes". He rushes out of the shop. Not for the car, but turned left and took off in an entirely different direction of the mobile across the way. Lance followed after out of the door, but went in the direction of the car. Cyrus was so far away at this point, that he could only

hear the sheer loud grunts of Lance's voice shouting at Sean, and possibly for him to come back.}

TEEN CYRUS: (He always shouts at Sean! Why does he always shout?)

{Cyrus thought of that to take his mind off of the heavy reigning predicament.}

TEEN CYRUS: Dad! Mom!...
BANG, BANG, BANG!
Dad! Mom! Dad! Mom!...
BANG, BANG, BANG!
Dad! Mom! Dad! Mom!...
BANG, BANG!
Dad! Mom!

{Cyrus had run all the way home, and began banging on the door as boisterously as he could. As he banged and banged at the door, he noticed the clock on the wall inside read 8:54 PM from outside. Exactly forty-eight minutes ago, he witnessed a murder.

His father was the one to answer to the aggressive banging on the front door.}

CYRUS'S FATHER: Son, son—what is it!? You okay?

TEEN CYRUS: Dad.

{He lunges and grabs on to his father. His father not thinking twice before grappling him back. Holding on as if to never let go again. His face worried, but vacant. Steady and strong. They hang on to one another for roughly fifteen seconds as a loud engine purring car comes out from Gernsheim. White lights pushing heavy. Cyrus heard it; his father felt it coming in his heart. His son was in trouble. He pushed Cyrus to the ground as the lights angled and routed towards them. The car stutters in front of the home. Out comes a pouring of fire. Rounds shutter up onto the porch. Hitting the front door and the surrounding area on the stoop. One bullet enters the right temple of Cyrus' Father. Another through the right lung. Then another into the right side of the stomach. And then into the right quadriceps. Another into the left lung. Then the left side of the stomach. The left shoulder twice. Bullets fire for another two or three seconds and stop before he finally falls to the ground. And the white light speeds off in a roar. Another few seconds pass before Cyrus lifts his head. He looks back over his left foot to see what he had already projected in his mind through the smoking of gun fire. His father had indeed been shot to death. He reaches down to his faint parent with his left hand. his head ringing in despair. A clogged feeling in his chest. His left fingers touch the left shoulder of his perished father.} —

CYRUS: uuuuuhh!!

{*Cyrus awakes from a nightmare wide-eyed and gasping for air. Halfway lifted off of his king size mattress. And places his left hand over the left side of his head. A sense of anxiety. Back into the night where he had blacked out from the crazed party. The night started to shift into morning as Cyrus sat on his bed.*}

CYRUS S1C3:
ELIZABETH'S AFFECTION

{Cyrus looks out at the wake of his window as the sky is of grey and blue. One leg crossed under him sitting on the edge of his expensively well quilted blankets.}

BUZZ...BUZZ...BUZZ

{His phone rings on the side of him on the bed. Ring may be an overstatement. No one uses a ringtone. The phone simply vibrates vigorously. Cyrus glares over at it and allows it to vibrate two to three more times before answering.}

CURTIS: You up?

{Cyrus takes a deep breath pretending he'd just awoke.}

CYRUS: Yes.

CURTIS: Okay, well I'm on my way over by the way.

CYRUS: Yeah, okay. (*What the hell happened last night?*)

CURTIS: Dude you are wild as fuck.

CYRUS: What? What do ya' mean—I didn't even do anything last night.

CURTIS: You did... drugs though. A lot. I tried to stop you. —
CYRUS: Like? —
CURTIS: But you know how you get.

CYRUS: Like... what kind?

CURTIS: Some cocaine, a hint of weed, and some alcohol. Dude you better slow down if you want to live till thirty.

CYRUS: Curtis—I know, man. And all the women?

CURTIS: Nah, you didn't do anything with them. You were rejecting them all... feverishly.

CYRUS: Yeah okay.

{Cyrus notices Curtis's choice of words, and chuckles.}

CYRUS: Why "feverishly"? Seems like a... very complex word. It's too early for big words.

CURTIS: ... I think it had something to do with Liz' —so what's up toda—

CYRUS: What?—Curtis, relax. I'm already under enough pressure as is. I don't need that hanging over my head right now. It's far too early in the morning for that.

CURTIS: Oh yeah, *you're* right, *my* bad. So what's the word today? Get your butt out of bed.

CYRUS: Huuh, I don't know. I don't have to be at the office today. You wanna just... come over here and hang around until I sober up? And then we'll figure things out from there and then?

CURTIS: Yeah, I'm already on my way, foo'! About two blocks away. I got food of course. Donuts, some coffee—

CYRUS: Come on, you know I don't do coffee.

CURTIS: You need to start.

CYRUS: ... nah not today.

CURTIS: Well...—

CYRUS: Are you driving and on your phone? You know that's dangerous right?

CURTIS: Oh, shut up.

CYRUS: Ahahaha.

CURTIS: Down the street. I shouldn't have to be buzzed in anymore; it's kind of pointless at this point. Everybody already knows who I am. Auggie just likes to give me a hard time.

CYRUS: Ahaha, well that is her job, "foo'". She just can't go letting any and everybody in, can she?

CURTIS: "Any and everybody"? Really? I've been

coming here for three years now. I'm not "any and everybody". She should know who I am by now.

Cyrus: Well, ahaha, she's got to do her job, man. I don't know what else to tell ya'. You want me to get you a key card—a pass key?—what do ya' want *me* to do?

CURTIS: Are you kidding me!? You need to save those excuses, bro!

CYRUS: Ahahahaha. Yeah okay, ahaha!

CURTIS: I'm outside. I'm hanging up. Buzz me in.

CYRUS: Alright, hang up.

{*Curtis bops his way into the lobby.*}

CURTIS: Hey, Auggie; how's it going?

AUGGIE: Hey, Curtis, how's it going?

CURTIS: Fine. But can you just let me in next time so I don't have to call Cyrus to buzz me in?

AUGGIE: Ahahaha.

CURTIS: No—seriously though. I'm here all the time. You guys know me here.

AUGGIE: We can't do that, Curtis.

CYRUS: Hm, just asking.—I'm just saying, I'm here just as much as Cyrus is.

AUGGIE: That may be true, Curtis, but you're not a resident.

CURTIS: Man! Why do red heads always have to give everyone a *hard* time!?

{Auggie just shakes her red head and laughs.}

{Curtis heads up the stairway west of the front desk of the vividly, glass filled condominium lobby. Curtis loved to take the stairs for some strange reason. Maybe because it gave him a sense of adventure. Or maybe just because of the light exercise. Though Cyrus lived on the second floor from the top floor. He traveled all the way up bearing a box and cups. He arrives at Cyrus' door, and so Cyrus opens up.}

CURTIS: I come bearing gifts.

CYRUS: Did you get my favorite?

CURTIS: Of course I did! "Caramel Glaze 'O' with Sprinkles!"

{*Curtis places the pink box of a dozen donuts and coffee on the glass coffee table in Cyrus's sitting room.*}

CURTIS: Your favorite.

CYRUS: Yes! Thanks, pal. How will I ever thank you enough?

CURTIS: So, what's on the agenda today?

CYRUS: Well, we both know what is first...

{*Curtis and Cyrus engage in video games for about two hours in "gaming time"—four hours in reality. Then a game of "who can chuck the most junk food", and a sitting of stand-up comedy. They grew exhausted, so Cyrus sits flat backed on the white sofa with little movement, while Curtis sits on the love seat the same.*}

CURTIS: Alright Cy', time to get out.

CYRUS: What!? We're having too much fun. We don't need to... go anyway—anywhere.

CURTIS: I got a date, and you do too. I told Elizabeth I was looking for someone to hang out with, you know, someone to romance, and she got me a date with one of her work friends or something.

CYRUS: So...

CURTIS: Ahm, yeah.

CYRUS: I'm guessing, Elizabeth is my date?

CURTIS: Hm? Yah. She says she wanted to hang out with you soon. I thought you guys discussed this at the party last night? —

CYRUS: Well you just lied, because I know she didn't say that. We were making out plans for next week not the following day.

CURTIS: Yah; well I asked her to go out with you, okay?

In plus, she probably wants some answers about why those hoes were following you out last night. Assuming you'd wanna answer to that.

{Cyrus stares faintly.}

CURTIS: Come on—stop it, dude. You know you want to go out with her anyway.

{Cyrus takes a deep breath.}

CYRUS: Whatever. I suppose it can't be helped. Right?

CURTIS: Nope. You gotta be ready by eight o'clock. We gotta be there by nine o'clock.

CYRUS: Yeah, well I'll be ready by '8:15'. Where's this "date" at though?

CURTIS: ... You're not doing anything right now though. And we're going to the State Carnival.

{Cyrus and Curtis head out to meet their dates at the State Carnival Grounds. They meet up with Elizabeth and her friend at the front gates at exactly 9:00 PM.}

CYRUS: Hi.

ELIZABETH: Hey, Cyrus.

{Elizabeth shines her smile at Curtis, and introduces him to her friend "Maddie". They all have small talk before deciding to break into couples. Elizabeth and Cyrus walking through the well-lit fair having small talk.}

ELIZABETH: So, how have you been? Anything new or...?

CYRUS: Uhm, no. Nothing new.

ELIZABETH: Oh. How's work been?

CYRUS: It's been good.

{Cyrus pretended to be enthused even with the ever-present awkwardness. The two eventually park their uneven spoken conversation and bodies along the fenced outskirts that oversee the entire carnival.}

CYRUS: Elizabeth, I have to tell you something... I...

hate to come off this way, because most women are the same, and they may think I'm weird.

{*They both blush and giggle.*}

CYRUS: But... I like the way your nose crinkles and your cheeks turn red when you smile and... or laugh. I like your long beautiful brunette hair, and your big green eyes, I just like you. More than just "average". I feel I've known you for so long, but... I know it's only been a year since we've really gotten to know each other better. I am... I have... fallen in love with you, Elizabeth. Now the question is, "are you the exemption to the norm? Or are you like all these other girls?"

ELIZABETH: What do you mean?

CYRUS: Well, a lot of women take what men tell them as passion, and use it against them. Dragging the guy's emotions through the mud. I just hope you're different, because I really feel you are.

ELIZABETH: Wow Cyrus. I... don't know what to say. You're so sweet!

CYRUS: ...Yeah.

ELIZABETH: I'm... speechless, honestly.

CYRUS: I want to show you something. Something that proves this is not an illusion. Something that shows you how much I care.

PAUSE!

THE CARNIVAL FREEZES

{*Cyrus waves his hand over the entire park after closing his eyes to focus on what he cares for most. Elizabeth's affection.*}

CYRUS S1C4:
WONDER-STRUCK

{*Elizabeth's eyes were glazed. Her lips agate. The possibility of what Cyrus had done seemed to be unbearable. She looked at the frozen Ferris wheel, then swiftly at Cyrus, then back to the frozen bodies all staged in front of her, for her, then back at Cyrus. Clearly, she was without a word or pitch.*}

CYRUS: It's a gift, from God himself.

{*Cyrus flashes his million-dollar smile with a slight arrogance.*}

ELIZABETH: But you...—people shouldn't be able to do that! What did you do? Is this some kind of trick!?

CYRUS: I wanted to show you who I am.

ELIZABETH: . . . Haha. This is crazy. Completely crazy.

How'd you do it!?

CYRUS: I know, I know. It's not a magic trick though; it's completely real—but Elizabeth... It's okay. I would never hurt you.

{Cyrus began to defend himself for no reason at all.}

CYRUS: I want you to know that. I... I just wanted to show you... I wanted to be completely open to you. Is that okay?

ELIZABETH: Yes, but do you know how much power you have in... just your hands? Who else knows you can do this!?

CYRUS: Just a few people... very close to me. Curtis included, of course.

ELIZABETH: I would have never guessed you carry such a heavy burden on your shoulders.

CYRUS: Let me help you.

ELIZABETH: What? And you should probably un-freeze all of this now.

CYRUS: Right. **PLAY!**

TIME PLAYS

CYRUS: I know. I know everything. I know about your father.

ELIZABETH: You "...know everything..." about? —

CYRUS: Your father.

{*Cyrus began to assume a smothering stance of conviction like he was pitching the "next big thing!"*}

ELIZABETH: How do you know that? What exactly do you plan to do about my father?

{*Elizabeth was merely offended Cyrus had taken the time to care more than she was accustomed to someone showing such interest.*}

ELIZABETH: Haha, you're gonna break him out of prison or something?

{A million-dollar smile never appeared so genuine.}

CYRUS: Well if I did that, we'd both be fugitives, and I would have to freeze time for forever.

ELIZABETH: What are you going to do? Time travel? Ahaha.—Ope! I'm sorry, no mean to laugh.

{Cyrus merely blushes.}

CYRUS: I was thinking along the lines of...

ELIZABETH: You can go back and fix that for me? Time travel? You can time travel?

CYRUS: I can, and I will go.

ELIZABETH: Well, you've done this much. If you could save my father... I don't know what to say. Thanks.

{The two stand in awe of one another. One based in reverence, the other in fear. But both enjoy a deep fond of respect.}

ELIZABETH: Can we talk about something else to-night? Just for tonight. I want to enjoy it.

{*This ends that conversation between the two, and they enjoy the rest of their night together. Enjoying various carnival activities without ever losing grip of visible joy and laughter.*}

{*Cyrus and Curtis meet up with each other at the gate they entered in.*}

CYRUS: So, how'd it go?

CURTIS: Eh, it was alright. She's a cool girl. Ya' know?

CYRUS: I guess.

{*They begin to walk and talk on the way to Cyrus's car.*}

CURTIS: How'd it go with Liz?

CYRUS: Oh, it was good. She's... amazing, I guess.

CURTIS: Just "good"?

CYRUS: Well, I showed her.

CURTIS: Showed her what? Your—

{*Curtis grotesquely gestures towards his genitalia.*}

CYRUS: No! No, stop!

CURTIS: Kidding! What'd you show her then?

CYRUS: What I can do?

CURTIS: You mean like...

CYRUS: Yep.

CURTIS: You serious—you did that?

CYRUS: I had to. I do not want there to be any secrets between us.

CURTIS: I think that is a secret you should have kept. Why did you show her?

CYRUS: I just told you why.

CURTIS: Come on, man. That's not the only reason. I know you better than that. You do things like this when you're about to do something really over the top for affection. You know, you don't have to... defend or protect everyone. Sometimes you gotta just let stuff be, man. I know how you feel about her, but...

CYRUS: ... Okay. I told her I would do something for her.

CURTIS: Stop being vague!

CYRUS: We'll talk about this on the way.

{*Curtis and Cyrus get into the slim white mobile, the opposite of his dark, moonlit vehicle. On their way back to Cyrus's condominium, there is a brief 5 or 6 minutes of silence before Cyrus continues his under-willed story.*}

CYRUS: I told her I would go back and save her father.

CURTIS: ... What do you mean? —

CYRUS: Like, go back. —

CURTIS: Go back where!? We're not getting any-where—where are you going back to?

CYRUS: In time.

CURTIS: ... so you mean like... time travel?

CYRUS: Yeah—yes, Curtis. Like time travel.

{Curtis's reaction was unevenly calm.}

CURTIS: ... you high, or? What are you smoking these days besides weed? You can do cool stuff with time, but when have you ever—

CYRUS: Just... relax. I can take it. I can do it, alright.

CURTIS: Yeah, you can. And kill yourself. And what year is this? I know... her father was arrested...—for some fucked up shit.

CYRUS: 2008.

CURTIS: ... Do you not know how much power that would take of you? That was like—what? 7 or 8 years ago? You might not make it back. Hell, you *might* not even make it *there*! You might tear yourself into a thousand pieces before you even make it there!

{*Cyrus sits one hand on the wheel in ignorance.*}

CURTIS: I know you want to impress her, but this is not the way to do it.

CYRUS: ...Well if you ever learn how to count, it was nine years ago. I'm doing this because I care for her. How long have I known Elizabeth Wilson?

CURTIS: Like a couple of years. But you don't know her *that* well. Like "Time travel to save your father from murdering his wife" well.

CYRUS: We have had our ups and downs over the last couple of years. I've seen her at her best, and I feel I know what her worst is. We've been around each other way more this year.

CURTIS: Yeah, like when that asshole she dated made her cry, because he was an asshole.

Do you really think this will change much of anything? For you? Not time alone, because we already know you're gonna fuck that up.

CYRUS: I don't know. But I'm gonna do this.

[*Four days later...*]

{*Cyrus trots into 'CYRUS Tower' and is again greeted by Rhonda Scott.*}

RHONDA: Hello, Cyrus. How are you doing this afternoon?

CYRUS: Oh I'm fine, Rhonda. Thank you very much. How are you this afternoon?

RHONDA: Well, I'm fine as well.

You have the 12:30 with Dispense Distributions.

{Cyrus lets off a distinctive grimace.}

CYRUS: Shit. Can these guys find someone else to flip and market that shit?

RHONDA: Well... they are having a hard time; that's why they came to you.

CYRUS: I suppose. How big's their team?

RHONDA: Uhh, I think I saw about... 5 or 6 of them.

CYRUS: Okay. Intercom "I'm on my way," please, could ya' Rhonda?

RHONDA: Sure! No problem, Cyrus. But hey, you look a little... "off" today. Everything alright?

CYRUS: Yes. I'm perfectly fine.

{With a convincing grin, had Cyrus. Rhonda looks at him with suspicion. But it passed rather quickly.}

RHONDA: Okay. Good luck in your meeting.

CYRUS: Thank you Rhonda. I'll see you soon after on my way out!

{*Cyrus heads up to the meeting room with Dispense Distributions.*}

CYRUS: Good afternoon, gentlemen! And lady. I certainly hope I haven't kept you all waiting too long! Do you enjoy the office space? You get the complimentary drinks we had sent for you?

DD MEMBER #1: It is most definitely fine, Mr. O'Brian, and the drinks were delightful. Thank you for having us. I suppose we should get started, shall we?

CYRUS: *Absolutely.* So, tell me, what are some of your goals with Dispense Distributions? Where do you see this brand in the next 5 years?

DD MEMBER #1: Most certainly, Mr. O'Brian, mass distribution of our brand of course. —

CYRUS: Of course, but can we be more specific? When and how will Dispense Distributions be mass producing? Who will be feeling the ultimate benefits of all Dispense Distributions has to offer? And how do we go about execution, huh?

{Cyrus preys on all of the members of Dispense Distributions before choosing his victim for questioning.}

CYRUS: You! You tell me—any ideas Mr... Mr... —

DD MEMBER #2: "Tantrinado", "Mr. Tantrinado", sir.

CYRUS: Tantrinado! Mr. Tantrinado, can you explain to me how we go about making "DD" a "well known family brand"? No, because you wouldn't be here if you did. Obviously, right? Allow me to put it this way everyone: The goal isn't to make the first big millions, but to sustain them. Sustainability is the key to success. How do we protect the brand after initial success to expand into new horizons and margins, right? Which one of you is the marketing director?

DD MEMBER #3: ME! Name's Pete. From Breeze Bright.

CYRUS: How ya' doin', Pete?

PETE FROM BREEZE BRIGHT: I'm fine, just trying to learn, ya' know?

CYRUS: That's great, Pete! And learn you will. That's why we're here, right? How much marketing planning execution do you do in one day to a week would you say, Pete?

PETE FROM BREEZE BRIGHT: I dunno... maybe an ad idea a couple weeks or so. Run it by "Mr. Boss-man" here, and we push it out to see who Is willing to market the ideas at a... productive rate. Sometimes we may get 1 idea to be sponsored. Other times, we get nothin'.

CYRUS: *Exactly*, Pete. You all hear what he said here!? Pete, I don't know you all that well, but let me just tell you what I've gathered, Pete: you tend to take, "no" for an answer. There's no "nos" in this industry. We don't take a damn "*no*" as a valid answer. 1 promo every two weeks? Come on, those are novice numbers! What are you a local plumber?

PETE FROM BREEZE BRIGHT: ...

CYRUS: No! Because if you were, I'm sure "*Mr. Boss-man*" over here would have never hired you. And what is your name —...

DD MEMBER #1: Clifton, thank you very much.

{Clifton's lower lip flips over his upper causing a frog like bulge in his chin. His eyes lowered in curiosity. He didn't seem too fond of Cyrus's egotistical demeanor. But... he needed Cyrus's help. So he will let him be.}

CYRUS: Clifton, two ads a week, at the very least! If you want results, you have to put in the money. Let's not be cheap here. A couple thousand on advertisement in two weeks' time, and I guarantee you a minimum return on investment, if it's all done properly of course with the right resources—don't worry, I can help you guys with that.

{Cyrus takes a look at his platinum plated watch. He seems to be in a rush. Understandable with what he has been planning since his last meeting with Elizabeth. He had scheduled another meeting with Elizabeth at the local coffee shop, "Frappes". They wanted to sort out the details of Cyrus's up and coming "trip".}

CYRUS: Alright! Can we agree on a number? From your books, and believe me, when I say I have seen this *hundreds of times* in my short, but not so short, successful career, I know what it's gonna cost: $1,056 per week with my 5% commissions rate, of course added on to that, and you will see a net profit of at least 8% in your first month with me. I am not predicting your investment future, that is just our bottom-line guarantee for our professional, top-tier marketing campaign assistance here at 'CYRUS Tower'. All of this okay with *you*, Clifton?

{Mr. Clifton seems gratefully surprised. His shoulders became leveled with his chin line. He takes a slight lean back in his chair to peer over to his associates and peers. They all seemed satisfied with Cyrus's presentation. More so based on his illustrious resume than his rushed and seemingly inconsiderate presentation. All members of Dispense Distributions looked back at Clifton with faces that said, "Take the deal!" So, Clifton looked back over to Cyrus. Took a pause and accepted the offer.}

MR CLIFTON: Let's do it.

CYRUS: Great! Alright. My assistant will be right in with you guys to get the paperwork done. I actually have to get going for another meeting here. Lady—you are wonderful, I got a lot of respect for you. Gentlemen, it is going to be my *utmost* pleasure to work with all of you, have a great day.

{Cyrus turns with one hair swoosh and leaves the room. The room silent in shock of how Cyrus built such a successful company with the lack of attention to rapport building.}

{Cyrus makes his way through the light of mid-day's rush hour. He arrives at Frappes just a couple minutes later than he wanted.

All of the local musicians hung out there to network for subjective acclamation to fame. It hadn't worked out too well for the majority of them. Maybe they had trouble promoting their brands? Also, some of them just lacked the necessary talents, or the image to succeed in the music industry. Plus, no major record labels looked at Double-City as a place to find the next great big thing.

Frappes was cream colored with outdated tables that looked like they came from the 50s. Very stylish for this community of individuals. Frappes always had quality business.

Cyrus spots Elizabeth with her face in a steaming coffee. Her hair slightly curled, and she wore a long-sleeved grey turtleneck that seemed to be just a couple of sizes too large. She wore a fashionable ring on her left middle finger. It clearly wasn't real, but it was cute on Elizabeth. She spots Cyrus up ahead and flashes her beautiful smile, ear to ear at him. Cyrus gives a slight smile, but his eyes said more. He breaks the connection and rushes over to her table.}

ELIZABETH: Hi, Cyrus!

CYRUS: Hi, Elizabeth.

ELIZABETH: You'd think someone who could control time would never be late.

CYRUS: Nice one.

ELIZABETH: I'm kidding. So, how are you doing? How are you going to do this?

CYRUS: Well, I've been thinking and hashing out the details, and then I realized, I don't know that much about the details.

ELIZABETH: Haha—... right. Okay, well, you know my father was wrongfully arrested for the death of my mother.

CYRUS: And what was the exact date of this...

ELIZABETH: The trial or? —

CYRUS: The... death—the incident.

ELIZABETH: Right. Well, it was February 7th, 2008.

CYRUS: And do you remember the exact time?

ELIZABETH: Yes. It was... *4:48 PM* when it happened. I remember, because I remember my father screaming from in my room. I was playing with my nail polish, and I was thinking about what time it was after I had just finished my homework. It was a Thursday night.

CYRUS: And the trial came relatively quickly, correct? Within a month?

ELIZABETH: Yeah, it was about 2 months, and they had a verdict.

CYRUS: Wow.

ELIZABETH: Yep. My father has been in prison since I was 13 years old. I just know it wasn't him. There was someone else there. I just know it!

{*Cyrus looks deep into Elizabeth's eyes not 28. to seduce her, but with curiosity. Cyrus was a master of this.*}

CYRUS: And what makes you think there was someone else there?

ELIZABETH: Well, my dad always had this routine: he'd always take a shower around 4:40PM. That way, after I finished my homework, he'd make time to spend with me. We had a maid, but she was downstairs because I remember she had the vacuum running. She couldn't have done it. She was just an older lady.

I know my parents; they were in love. There's no way my dad would harm my mom.

{*Cyrus tried to assure Elizabeth he believed every word with his eyes. He was a master at this, but he still had more questions. But he chose to not ask them to not rattle Elizabeth from the already unsettling interrogation.*}

CYRUS: Elizabeth, I can do this. Don't worry, I will make this all right. I will find out who really did this. So you know, I don't know exactly what this will do to our current present time. I've never traveled back this far. So...

{*Cyrus showed a sense of concern.*}

ELIZABETH: But what about your father?

{*Cyrus turns his head downward and to the left swiftly to disapprove of the question Elizabeth had asked of him. Pretending to be searching in his inner pocket for something other than comfort.*}

CYRUS: You know about my father?

ELIZABETH: Well, you know about mine...

CYRUS: Don't worry about me. This is all about you. Because like I've said... I have never gone back this far, and I don't know if I will ever be able to do it again. And if I do this, I want it to be for the right reasons.

{*There was now a silence. Elizabeth didn't understand Cyrus. She never could. The only thing she knew for sure about him, was he truly had a great heart.*}

CYRUS: Alright.

{*Cyrus stands up planning his exit.*}

ELIZABETH: You're going?

CYRUS: Yeah. I have to finish prepping. I'm going tomorrow night. Curtis has been helping me. We've watched enough detective shows in the last few days for a lifetime. We've learned a lot about being "true de-tectives", ahaha.

ELIZABETH: Well, okay. Thank you. Oh! Here's the address...

{*Liz slides a small, folded piece of lined paper across the diner table. Cyrus picks it up.*}

ELIZABETH: From... where I lived as a kid.

CYRUS: You're welcome.

{*The next night, Cyrus and Curtis are at Cyrus's condo finally getting ready for Cyrus to make the long trip back in time.*}

CURTIS: You're nuts.

CYRUS: I'm all packed and ready to go. I think I'm gon-na miss you, my friend.

CURTIS: Yeah, yeah; you just make it back in one piece. And you didn't pack anything. It's not a vacation.

CYRUS: Got it... right.

CURTIS: So how do you know this is gonna work? I still don't understand.

CYRUS: Well, I don't know why, but my powers have been really peaking lately. I've been feeling like I can do anything lately. I don't know why. You know those time gaps I have?

CURTIS: Yeah, when you can't use your powers after you've juiced out.

CYRUS: None of it. Not 5 minutes, not 3 minutes. No lag time.

CURTIS: Ahuh, and is this a certainty or just your ego again?

CYRUS: ... I can do this. I know it.

{*Curtis rests his case.*}

CURTIS: Alright. I'm gonna miss you, Cy'.

CYRUS: I'm gonna miss you as well. Alright. I'm gonna sit her for about 30 minutes to focus on the year 2008. I need to focus to make sure I hit the nail on the head and not overshoot or undershoot.

CURTIS: Shouldn't be too hard. 2008 was a pretty good year.

CYRUS: ... Yeah it was, wasn't it? I think guys going away from the boot cut era was the best thing for our generation.

CURTIS: Yeah. And social media and the internet really started to build traction. —

CYRUS: Right. There were previous smaller social networks n'things, but... none were like—

CURTIS: Yeah.

CYRUS: What we have today.

Alright, I'm gonna focus here.

CURTIS: Alright. Wait, how do I know you're still alive and didn't get pixelated?

CYRUS: ... I don't know—would you just wait and see!?

CURTIS: Alright. Good luck, man.

CYRUS: ... Thank you.

{*Thirty minutes of silence pass. Curtis sits quietly on his cell phone the entire time in the living room. While Cyrus stands in between the doorway to his master bedroom facing outward towards the higher-leveled greeting area past the living room with stairs upward into the loft area of the condominium to the right of him. After thirty minutes, it was time. Cyrus shouted abruptly. Causing Curtis's head to make a sharp turn toward where Cyrus stood. A huge spectrum of plasma ensues in the condo removing Cyrus.*}

CYRUS: **REWIND!**

TIME REWINDS [The Year 2008]

{*A huge spectrum of plasma and gas introduces Cyrus to a sidewalk at the peak of the day in an upper-middle class neighborhood. Dropping Cyrus on his back side with a slight thud. Not harsh enough to fracture anything in the buttocks or lower spinal columns. Maybe harsh enough to jam a shoulder into its socket*} *bracing himself as he landed on his backside. Nothing was fractured. The homes on the avenue resembled a familiarity as Cyrus grimaced and looked down over his feet ahead of him. Then, rotating his neck around the collar of his black pea-coat that was made of an expensive silk inner, and cotton outer combination. So the collar made a sound as Cyrus rotated over his head over his right shoulder. His hair glowing the sun's rays as he spots a child around the age of 13-15 racing on his bike on the parallel sidewalk behind him. He wore blue shorts, a light grey tee shirt with a blue cap to the back. Mid to high level socks were pretty popular in 2008. The bicycle was red. There was a hollering—a screaming behind the boy from a girl who appeared to be slightly younger. She wore dark jeans and a white tee shirt with her brunette hair flowing above and behind her shoulders. The wind blew Northeast revealing her face. She appeared to be having a great time chasing after the boy. Cyrus then spotted a tree that looked familiar the two children passed at a high, yet ordinary, speed. The tree was so light and golden. Old beyond belief with vivid splits in the wood vertically in zig-zag motions. Cyrus realized he had been here plenty of times as he looked forward of him again over his feet to the other parallel side as he lay next to a tree on the middle island strip separating two sides of the avenue. A sky-blue colored home with white in its mixture. Maroon colors trimmed the pillars and beak of the home. Cyrus stands as the sun glared from the Northeast now causing the grimace on Cyrus's face. He rushes over to the familiar home dusting off his white tee shirt under his coat which he didn't need because of the weather conditions seemed to be that of later spring. He hopped up the stairs which were also maroon colored and wooden. They made a bouncing sound as he skipped toward the door of the long horizontal porch. Ringing the doorbell and awaiting the residents. A male around the age of 43 comes to the door in a white wife beater and pajama pants that looked just like a checkerboard. He had serious five o'clock shadow with grays through his beard, and the front of his hair was widowed.}*

CYRUS: Hi, how's it going, sir?

HOME RESIDENT: How may I help you?

CYRUS: Well, I was wondering if your son Curtis were here. Is he?

HOME RESIDENT: What do you want with my son? What'd he do?

CYRUS: Oh he's not in any trouble, sir. I'm just an old friend. Mr. Loans, it's me, "Cyrus".

CURTIS'S FATHER: What?

CYRUS: It's me, "Cyrus O'Brian."

{Mr. Loans took a long look at Cyrus, squinted his face up in a sour form, and realized it was indeed 'Cyrus O'Brian'.}

MR. LOANS: My God!... What the *hell* did you do this time?

CYRUS S1C5: FAMILIAR COMPANY

MR. LOANS: Jesus, Cyrus, what have you done this time?

CURTIS?

{*Mr. Loans diverts his attention away to call upon his son. But his eyes stayed on Cyrus.*}

MR. LOANS: CURTIS!

YOUNG CURTIS: Yes, Dad?

MR. LOANS: Come down here and see this, son!

{*Mr. Loans still looking up and down the frame of Cyrus. Trying to make sense of what Cyrus has done. a "Young Curtis" comes running down the staircase*} *aligned about 8 feet away just slightly right of the front door from the outside's perspective. The staircase is a dark chocolate color with faded wood in plenty of spots. Diversifying the color scheme of the staircase. This staircase was beyond aged. As Curtis bounced down the case with young energy, the steps creaked with every bounce. Curtis appeared from above wearing faded blue pajama bottoms to the point where they appeared white. They were the appropriate size. He wore dark grey socks with a dark grey top. The sleeves of the short sleeve shirt were black, or navy blue. Curtis wore a fauxhawk back in 2008 with too much gel up top causing spikes with his dyed hair.}*

YOUNG CURTIS: Yeah, Dad?

{Mr. Loans looked back over his left shoulder down at a fresh 14-year-old Curtis who had not fully grown into his current height. And motions his un-shaved five o'clock shadow toward Cyrus with widened eyes. He stumbled over his next worded expression.}

MR. LOANS: Would you look at this?

YOUNG CURTIS: What?

{Young Curtis looks at Cyrus with squinted confusion as in not knowing what his father would get out

of simply telling him to look at a complete stranger standing in his doorway.}

MR. LOANS: ... Look.

{Curtis looked at the stranger again a little deeper, but not expecting to get a new result out of repetition. Curtis took a step toward him and squinted his eyes even harder sticking his neck out as conclusions started to form in his head.}

YOUNG CURTIS: Wait a minute... Cyrus!?

{A huge wide mouthed smile appeared on Curtis's face.}

YOUNG CURTIS: HOLY SHIT! —

MR. LOANS: Ah—CURTIS!

YOUNG CURTIS: Sorry, Dad.

{Curtis stayed in the moment.}

YOUNG CURTIS: What did you do!?

MR. LOANS: This is too much for me. Cyrus—"Adult Cyrus", I don't even wanna know. Could you take Curtis down to the diner for some lunch? Take my car.

{Mr. Loans grabs his car keys from atop the old wooden dresser in the hallway next to the staircase. It had a large white lilac covering on it. He tosses his keys to Cyrus and walks back over near him.}

MR. LOANS: You guys figure it out.

Curtis, go get dressed. I've got to get ready to head out with your mom. You know how long she takes. We've got to make sure you have groceries for tomorrow. Now we don't have to hire a babysitter.

{Curtis turns and races up the stairs slapping his hands on some of the steps as he ran up. Mr. Loans turns and looks at Cyrus again with his head slightly nodded with his hands in his checkered pockets. Cyrus still standing in the doorway with his hands in his pockets as well. There was still, a silence as if Cyrus was in anticipation of the next questions, but...}

MR. LOANS: Ahh I don't wanna know.

{Mr. Loans turns away as he makes this statement,

but, there was one more critical question he had to ask before allowing his son to run off with an assuming stranger with some credibility.}

MR. LOANS: You're not like a... a... evil clone, are you?

CYRUS: ... No.

{And Mr. Loans heads down the hallway to the left of the stairway.}

MR. LOANS: Bring him back! His mother won't be happy if you kidnapped em'. I would.

{Adult Cyrus and Curtis head down to the 'Orch Diner' in the heart of the neighborhood just a few blocks from the Loan's household. The plaza was always packed with moving vehicles, and young teens looking to get into trouble. They generally hung out on their bicycles at the edge of the plaza. Curtis was relatively silent on the drive over still in shock of Adult Cyrus before him. He just stared at him for prolonged stints multiple times on the way.}

CYRUS: Curtis would ya' stop staring!? You're freakin' me out!

YOUNG CURTIS: I'm freaking you out?

{Considering Cyrus knew he traveled back in time 9 years, and is now taking his best friend for food, not because they wanted to hang out, but because Curtis needed a "Parent or Guardian" present, his case of being "freaked out" was not benign.

They pull into the lot in front of the diner in the bright navy-blue car in the broad day of rush hour. The diner had a tan concrete design with huge windows up front allowing you to see from front to back of the diner, if it were dark out.}

YOUNG CURTIS: It's kind of weird seeing you drive my dad's car. Actually, it's weird seeing you driving at all. Actually, it's just weird seeing you as an adult!

CYRUS: Let's go.

{They both hop out of the appearing freshly cleaned car, and head into the diner. There was just one couple in their late thirties ahead of them in line to order food. Both dressed like the snobby adults that taught them in Junior High School that felt they were 10 years younger than what they actually were. The male, with grays through his hair, always wanted you to call him by his first name, and the woman, strawberry blonde,

would get highly offended if you ever mentioned her personal relationship life. Nonetheless, the students already assumed these two dated.}

CYRUS: What do you want to eat?

YOUNG CURTIS: Uhm, let me get the buffalo hoagie, I think. That's good. But I kinda want the cheese steak sandwich.

{Cyrus slowly looks over down at Young Curtis with a grueling expression in ultimate realization of how difficult this day was going to be with a teenage Curtis.}

YOUNG CURTIS: I'll just take the buffalo hoagie.

CYRUS: You sure?

YOUNG CURTIS: ... Yeah?

{Cyrus and Young Curtis found a table, sit and eat before the pestering starts as Curtis stuffs his mouth with his hoagie.}

YOUNG CURTIS: So, how'd you do it? What did you do?

CYRUS: I've time traveled. Quite obvious.

YOUNG CURTIS: You're from the future; when did you learn how to rewind time?

{*Cyrus gets a bit uncomfortable before answering the question.*}

CYRUS: ...16. It was 16.

YOUNG CURTIS: That's so cool.

CYRUS: You know you can't tell "Me"—... "Younger Me" about this, right?

YOUNG CURTIS: Of course! Something about, "it will affect our time we're in..." somehow. So why did you come to me? I'm just a teenager. Yep, worked hard for these years. You have all this power... why me? Why do you need anyone?

{*Cyrus takes a look around the clustered diner before leaning in, lowering his tone to reach Curtis.*}

CYRUS: I'm going to need your help. I can't exactly

get a hotel. There can be no records that I was here. Especially since I'm all juiced out, I need to lay as low as possible.

{*Curtis is still bouncing around a bit and talking with his mouth full.*}

YOUNG CURTIS: So why are you here? In 2008?

CYRUS: It's for a woman I met. Her name is "Elizabeth".

{*Young Curtis looks up at Cyrus with a face full of hoagie sauce and puffed cheeks. He shakes his head and goes back into his hoagie.*}

YOUNG CURTIS: You were always a sucker for vagina.

CYRUS: ... What man isn't?

YOUNG CURTIS: So, what do you need me to do?

CYRUS: I'm going to need a place to stay. I'll have to talk to your father when we get back to the house. Borrowing his car is also going to have to be a thing. Curtis, seriously, no one can know I'm here. If I'm spotted, it's over. I can't 'pause' or 'rewind' time at the moment. Traveling this far... I'm done. Powers are "poofed!"

YOUNG CURTIS: Where does this "Elizabeth" stay?

CYRUS: She lives west of the city in the suburbs out there past West Highway. You know, It's her parents place. Her father was imprisoned for the murder of her mother when she was 12. —

YOUNG CURTIS: Wait, you're 13 right now though.

CYRUS: ... Yeah, what's your point?

YOUNG CURTIS: You're dating women younger than you!?

CYRUS: It's different when you're an adult, Curt'.—

YOUNG CURTIS: Ewww, you're a creeper!

{*Cyrus scours the room hoping no one heard Curtis. It was already the time in society where it was becoming odd for adults to be around teens in 2008. It was odd before, but the media made it a point back in 2006 to make sure these "predators" were well accounted for. Every little action could be assuming serious charges on a before-mentioned, clean slate. An adult dining with a 14-year-old child could raise red flags to some. Curtis shouting "creeper" wouldn't help very much.}*

CYRUS: Would you keep it down!? Jesus. She's turning 13!

YOUNG CURTIS: But you're turning 14, ewwww!

{Cyrus rolls his eyes.}

CYRUS: Fucking kids.

{Cyrus takes a look at his watch. Just as a notion that he would be heavily keeping track of time while he was there.}

CYRUS: I'm going to find out who really did it. She doesn't believe it was her father. I'm going to find out who murdered her mother and have them arrested.

YOUNG CURTIS: When does this happen?

CYRUS: In exactly... 5 Days from now. I wish I could have gotten a bit closer to the date.

YOUNG CURTIS: Why didn't you?

CYRUS: I wish it were that simple. But this time travel stuff is like... it feels like a catapult the further back I go. It's very hard to hit the target. Especially since this is my first time ever doing a massive time leap like this one.

{*Curtis lets out an obnoxious belch.*}

CYRUS: You done?

YOUNG CURTIS: So what do you want to do until then?

CYRUS: I'll just have to lay low.

{*Cyrus throws a tip down on the table left of his plate. He had a cold chicken sandwich, white bread with lots of lettuce. It was the signature sandwich at Orch Diner.*}

CYRUS: Think you can go 5 days without seeing 'Me'?

YOUNG CURTIS: Yeah? Why wouldn't I be able to?

{The next morning, Cyrus sat on the Mayan designed sofa with his white tee shirt on and pajamas that were two sizes too wide. They belonged to Mr. Loans. An eaten bowl of cinnamon cereal in front of him. The cinnamon was still swirling in the milk. Cyrus was lactose-intolerant. He called eating all the cereal pieces in the bowl, "finished".

It was a bright Sunday morning outside, but the lighting inside the Loans household was always dim and drab. The drapery east of the sofa was grey and white. Odd being that the Loans family were not drab people.}

MR. LOANS: Hey Cyrus I'm going to run some errands. A friend needs help moving on the South Side like I told ya'. Think you'll be alright here? We'll be out all day.

{Cyrus turns over his left shoulder towards the front door with a huge grin where Mr. Loans stood with a grey skull cap a size too big for his head, the jacket too large, and a scarf. It was the Spring, but the weather is beyond unpredictable around Double-City. Cold should always be expected.}

CYRUS: Absolutely. No problem.

MR. LOANS: Keep an eye on the kid?

CYRUS: Sure thing.

MR. LOANS: Honey! Let's go!

MRS. LOANS: Coming!

{*Mrs. Loans comes running down the stairs in a pair of fitted red jeans. A white-collar shirt, with a belt with silver buckle holes all around the entire black design. She had dark brown hair, and usually always wore her hair down, because she was always prepared to make an impression. Cyrus rarely saw Mrs. Loans unprepared. She rushed for her black coat hanging near the front door.*}

MR. LOANS: See ya' later, Cy'.

MRS. LOANS: Good-bye, Cyrus!

CYRUS: See you guys later.

{*Cyrus turns back to the silver-trimmed 50"-inch television which had some bulk on the backside. As he begins to catch up on weekly trends on the TV, about 6- or 7-minutes pass before he hears yelling from a pitchy voice coming from outside of the front door. Knocking and doorbell ringing. It was definitely a teen. Around Curtis's age. A familiar voice.*}

TEENAGE KID: CURTIS! YOO-HOO! I'M HERE! COME TO THE DOOR!

{*Cyrus turns and hops up from the sofa with a striking pulse through his blood. He definitely recognized the voice, because it must have been his own.*}

CYRUS: Oh shit.

CYRUS S1C6: DOWN MEMORY LANE

CYRUS: What the hell did you do!?

{*Cyrus whispers aggressively with an egregious tone as Young Curtis comes bouncing down the stairs barefoot wearing his Saturday morning pj's.*}

YOUNG CURTIS: What!?

{*Curtis whispers back at Cyrus in a defensive tone.*}

CYRUS: What the fuck do you mean, "What!?"

YOUNG CURTIS: Hey, watch your mouth!

{*Cyrus shows how much he expected such irritation being haggled by a teenager. Not just on his choice of words, but the fact Curtis was dismissive and*

deliberately going against his wishes.
Curtis seemed to be on his way to opening the front door.}

CYRUS: Don't you dare! And keep your tone down before he hears us!

{*The voice from outside of the door starts to grow curious.*}

THE VOICE: Hey, Curtis!? What's takin' so long!?

{*Cyrus's gaze narrows heavier at Young Curtis standing midway down the stairwell holding on to the rail with his right hand. Curtis seems to be in a dilemma of some sort. Matching Cyrus's gaze with his own. Should he fire towards the front door with lesser regard to Cyrus than he'd already shown? Or should he continue to listen to the bickering of Cyrus.*}

CYRUS: *Don't you dare.*

Why would you invite him over!?

YOUNG CURTIS: I don't know. He's my friend?

{*Cyrus performs a quick spin in frustration flipping and holding his head murmuring swear words to himself.*}

CYRUS: Did you tell him I was here?

{*Curtis finishes his jog down the stairwell with his chest facing the front door, and his head facing Cyrus in the hallway to the side of the stairway.*}

YOUNG CURTIS: No.

CYRUS: Good. Keep it that way! Get rid of him.

YOUNG CURTIS: No.

{*Cyrus throws another fit.*}

CYRUS: What the fuck!!

YOUNG CURTIS: Language!

CYRUS: Shut—shut the fuck up! Get the fuck out of here!

YOUNG CURTIS: I live here.

CYRUS: Your parents are gone, so I'm the adult here, so I'm in charge! Now... Now go back upstairs!

YOUNG CURTIS: No.

{Cyrus now exasperated, flops his arms at his sides.}

CYRUS: Why? Why would you tell him to come here?

YOUNG CURTIS: Because we already made plans to go to the mall today before you showed up!

THE VOICE: Hey! You gonna open the door any time soon!? My balls are starting to go cold out here!

{Cyrus runs over to Curtis and grabs hold of his shoulders with both hands forcing Young Curtis to focus on his eyes and his words.}

CYRUS: Alright. Here's the plan: I'm going to sneak out the back door. Don't say a god damn word about me, you understand? Anything you say could possibly alter the entire existence of both our timelines. Got it?

YOUNG CURTIS: Alright, alright. Just go!

{*Cyrus takes a look over at the front door, and then back to Curtis before affirming.*}

CYRUS: ... Alright. I trust you.

{*Cyrus takes off as quickly possible out the back door through the kitchen down the hall. Curtis turns and finally opens the door. When he opened the door, there stood the spitting image of Cyrus. It was 'Young Cyrus'.*}

YOUNG CYRUS: Damn it! What were you doing? Jerking off!?

YOUNG CURTIS: No. I was just... sleeping and didn't sleep with any clothes on.

YOUNG CYRUS: When did you start doing that? That's my thing.

YOUNG CURTIS: I'm gonna slip on some clothes, and then we can go.

YOUNG CYRUS: Well, alright, hurry the hell up! I've

got girls to impress! I'm coming in. It's cold as balls out there!

[At the Double-City Mall...]

{*The Double-City Mall was the main attraction of the community for wandering teens whose hormones had grown quite rampant. The urge for the opposite sexes to explore their confidence and personalities. Young Cyrus and Curtis are waiting in a very busy line at the food court. These lines aren't really lines, as teens are grouped around in their social circles chatting up a storm. Overgrown hair on their heads, and acne infested. The food court music above playing today's hottest tunes to keep patrons pleased as they wait.*

Adult Cyrus peers from behind a decorative plant across from the food court wearing a heavy set of shades. Trusting a teenager with the fate of his existence wasn't something he could leave unsupervised. Adult Cyrus also followed the boys into the shoe store, continuously walking past the front entrance. And into the urban clothing store for young adults where he pretended to shop for his "preteen child".}

CUSTOMER CLERK REP: Excuse me, sir, is there anything I can help you find today?

ADULT CYRUS: No, no. Just looking.

{*The Customer Clerk was red headed wearing a maroon collar shirt with her hair tied back. She had the most beautiful smile and freckles. She was about Cyrus's age. Which confused her as to how Cyrus somehow already had a teenage child he would be shopping urban wear for. Maybe Cyrus just didn't look like the urban wear type. The men's formal wear clothing department was down the way. She wore the expression vividly, but best to give all customers the same satisfactory service.*}

CUSTOMER CLERK: Right. Well, Are you... —

CYRUS: God damn it! I said, "I got it!"

{*Cyrus whispers ferociously again.*}

CUSTOMER CLERK: ... Sor-ry?

{*A few of the customers took notice to the outburst from Cyrus. Including Curtis who peered and noticed Adult Cyrus. Minutes later, Young Curtis and Young Cyrus head out of the department store. Curtis starts to pat around his clothing as though he'd forgotten something. He didn't forget anything.*}

YOUNG CURTIS: Oh, damn it. I forgot my wallet on that seat. Be right back.

{*Young Curtis jogs back into the department store and waits for his friend to turn his attention elsewhere before running over to address Adult Cyrus.*}

YOUNG CURTIS: What are you doing here!?

ADULT CYRUS: I'm... shopping?

YOUNG CURTIS: Cut the crap! You're spying on me!

ADULT CYRUS: ... Would *you* trust *your* existence in the hands of a teenager with too much gel in his fauxhawk? I'm sorry I never had the nerve to tell you that fauxhawk never made you look cool.

YOUNG CURTIS: Considering I'm a teenager... yeah. And wow, really? I always thought you thought my fauxhawk was cool!

ADULT CYRUS: You—

YOUNG CURTIS: I trust myself with my *own* life. So yes.

ADULT CYRUS: You just make sure you don't say anything.

YOUNG CURTIS: I won't! Geez, man. How many times do I have to say it?

ADULT CYRUS: ... Okay, I have to admit I was a little bored sitting at home.

Curtis... *older* Curtis and I watched a lot of detective shows and movies before I got here. Gotta practice if I wanna catch a *real* killer, ya' know?

YOUNG CURTIS: Just... go back home. I'll catch up with you when I get back.

ADULT CYRUS: Ahh, I think I'm going to patrol the city a little more. I kind of miss the year 2008.

YOUNG CURTIS: Okay, you do that. Just don't get caught.

{*Young Curtis runs back out of the department store to catch up with Young Cyrus. Leaving Adult Cyrus stuck in wonder of the boyish energy he once had which acted as a Pied Piper for trailing thoughts he'd been having since being back in the year 2008.*}

{*Cyrus goes for a drive. He stops the car 10 blocks West of the mall outside of a Junior High/Senior High School. One side was a Junior High, the right side was a Senior High. There was a long high fence protecting the outside from the football field. Cyrus sat there in the car upright and still. Daydreaming about days as a teenager; the mistakes he made back then laid heavy on his mind. Those grounds outside of the school made him feel as though he would now be reliving those moments. He could feel them on his skin. This was where he attended school. Junior and Senior High School. It was cloudy above now as Cyrus sat for 15 - 20 minutes before he drove off and visited a small Ethiopian restaurant being run out of a home a few blocks south of the school. The house had a small porch with one step to the left of the small concrete porch which led up to the front door which was bright orange wood. It was protected by a screen door that could have used a good cleaning. Cyrus still wearing shades to protect his identity, walked up to the front screen door and he knocks and waits. This is when Cyrus notices the drizzling the skies gave way to.*}

HOMEOWNER: Hello? How can I help you?

{*A woman with a heavy accent yells lightly from behind the door before opening. The creaking crevice at the corners of the door folded and unveiled a familiar face.*}

CYRUS: Hi, how are ya'? Can I have a plate of collard greens and extra plantains, please?

{The woman looks on from behind the screen with her neck straight, and face forward. She had twists in her hair. Some were light brown, and the others black. She had wide brown eyes, and wore an apron with a generic holiday turkey décor centered in the middle below her waist.}

THE WOMAN: You want African food?

CYRUS: Yes, ma'am. That's what I'm here for.

{Cyrus flashed his classic grin.}

THE WOMAN: ... What a white man like you doin' over here getting African food?

CYRUS: I just came from the city. I heard you have some of the best food around is all.

THE WOMAN: Hm. Alright. You know it's spicy, right?

CYRUS: Yes, ma'am. I use to —... Yes ma'am.

THE WOMAN: Alright. It'll be about 20 - 30 minutes. $13, please.

{*Cyrus takes the money from his inner coat pocket, and the woman reaches from behind the screen door. Which also creaked. She goes back in backwards letting the screen door bungee itself closed behind her. Cyrus jogs back to sit in the car in the driveway. He started thinking back again...*}

YOUNG CYRUS: Dad? Where are we?

CYRUS'S FATHER: I heard there was a good restaurant here.

YOUNG CYRUS: But this is a house! I don't see a restaurant.

CYRUS'S FATHER: The house is the restaurant, son. Come on, let's check it out.

{*Young Cyrus and his father go up to the door and order.*}

CYRUS'S FATHER: Hi! Can I have your collard greens, please. With extra plantains.

THE WOMAN: You know it's spicy, right?

CYRUS'S FATHER: Yes, I'm aware. And a small plate for my son here too.

THE WOMAN: We only have one size.

CYRUS'S FATHER: ...Hmmm, well I think we'll share then.

{*The Woman took a good look at Young Cyrus. Surveying the persona of a young white male.*}

THE WOMAN: Okay. 30 minutes, please.

CYRUS'S FATHER: Thank you.

[17 minutes later back in current time...]

THE WOMAN: SIR!

{*The woman was waving at Cyrus from the porch behind the screen door to not get wet from the rain with a plastic bag that read, "Thank You" all around it with to-go boxes on the inside. Cyrus notices her abruptly out of his dream and hops out of the car and skips through the rain that had now really picked up*} *its intensity in 17 minute's time. He approaches the woman as his suede like coffee bean shoes slapped the cracked concrete.}*

CYRUS: Thank you so much!

THE WOMAN: Looking like it's startin' to rain, ain't it?

CYRUS: ... Yes, it does. Thank you.

{Cyrus turns to start back his way to the car.}

THE WOMAN: You know you only the second white man to come over here, right?

{Cyrus turns back slowly.}

CYRUS: Really?

THE WOMAN: Yeah, some man and his son come by for the same plate. You look just like that boy. Been coming by for 2-a-3 years.

CYRUS: Really? Wow, haha. I guess... us city yuppies

are finding all the good spots again.

{*The woman's face has gone serious.*}

THE WOMAN: I don't believe in coincidence.

{*As the silence now faults below the slow drizzling rain drops that fall sparingly.*}

THE WOMAN: You better get going before the rain mess up that pretty hair of yours.

{*Cyrus turns to walk away slowly. Then stops. He turns back around to her. She folds her arms and shakes her head left to right as the screen door was being restricted by her standing. Constantly making that recoiling noise.*}

THE WOMAN: I won't say nothin'. I just hope it ain't black magic you messin' with. You might want to do somethin' with that mole. It gave you away.

CYRUS: Right. No... black magic. Enjoy the rest of your day.

{*Cyrus hops back into the car and drives off. He has*}

another thought, then another, and then another of the past...}

THE WOMAN: You are my only white customer, you know that!?

CYRUS'S FATHER: Why am I not surprised, haha.

THE WOMAN: AHAHAHAHAHA! My name is "Nadi".

CYRUS'S FATHER: I'm Alex. This is Cyrus.

NADI: Hi, Cyrus! Ahahaha! Well thank you for coming! Come back, please!

ALEX O'BRIAN: Oh we'll be back as usual, ahaha. Thanks, "Na-dee". Did I say that, right? Sorry if I butchered that, ahaha.

NADI: No, you're close. It's *"Nadi"*.

ALEX O'BRIAN: *"NA•DI"*...

NADI: Yes, *"Nadi"*.

Thanks for coming, alright? I'll see you all later!

ALEX O'BRIAN: Alright, I'll see you later.

{Tears slowly stream down Cyrus's face under his dark shades he still wore as he drove down the cracked road causing his body to bounce left and right at slow steady rhythms. He reaches into his left coat pocket and takes out a capsule of painkillers. He twists it open, pops two, and continues the ride.}

CYRUS S1C7: OUT OF OPTIONS AND OUT OF TIME

{*Cyrus pulls into the paved driveway to the left of the Loan's Family porch. A large vibrant green bush sits at the corner of the bottom right of the porch and to the left of the beautifully paved driveway. Curtis was awaiting on the edge of the walkway to the porch near the lawn. Watching as Cyrus parks the car. Lights on the car are on, so Cyrus gets sight of Curtis watching him pull in. The rain had subsided just before darkness completely falls. Cyrus exits.*}

YOUNG CURTIS: Where have you been?

CYRUS: Out. Just... taking a look around, is all.

YOUNG CURTIS: Aren't you worried someone will see you? You're just roaming around?

CYRUS: Yeah, I am.

{*Cyrus walks over to Curtis giving his "children's answer" to all of Curtis's questions. Adults generally did not feel the need to explain actions concerning their being to children. One hand in his coat pocket, and the other holding his to-go boxes. His left hand fiddling the cap of the painkillers in his left pocket. He rests over on the porch steps, sits his plate down next to him.*}

YOUNG CURTIS: Whatcha got?

CYRUS: Just... some food. Didn't you eat?

YOUNG CURTIS: Yeah. Just curious.

{*Cyrus observes Curtis like an 8th Grade science class student does a frog before slicing it open.*}

CYRUS: How does it feel? Having all that energy? Still being a kid?

{*Curtis walks over to take a seat next to Cyrus on the creaking staircase.*}

YOUNG CURTIS: I don't know. I've only been a kid so...

CYRUS: Savior every moment of being a kid. Being an adult is not all it's cracked up to be.

YOUNG CURTIS: Psht, yeah, okay. I'm over being told what to do. I just want to start my real life.

CYRUS: ... What do you think life is?

CURTIS: I don't know. But I know it's not this.

CYRUS: ... this is life, Curtis. You're young; live it up.

YOUNG CURTIS: Wait a minute, are you foreshadowing me?

{*Cyrus let off a sarcastic snicker.*}

CYRUS: You just learned that word? You're in the— what, 7th or 8th grade? 2008...

YOUNG CURTIS: I'm in the 8th.

{Cyrus nods in confirmation.}

YOUNG CURTIS: So what am I doing now? Well, in the future?

CYRUS: ... You know I can't tell you that—come on, now. But what I can tell you... we're still really good friends.

{There's that assuring grin again. He also rubs his left hand across Curtis's fauxhawk. Curtis didn't like it, but he didn't ruin the current bond by commenting on the damage that could have been done.}

YOUNG CURTIS: You seem so much... different though.

CYRUS: I am. But you've stuck with me every step of the way.

{Cyrus titers on how to say what he wanted next without giving away what he shouldn't.}

CYRUS: ... Something happened.

{There's a silence in conversation. You can hear the chirping of critters after the rain.}

CYRUS: You're still the best friend I've ever had. Just promise me... you will understand. In a few years... promise me you'll understand.

{Young Curtis was baffled, but this had to be more foreshadowing.}

YOUNG CURTIS: "Understand"? Understand what?

{Cyrus smiles at Curtis.}

CYRUS: Just...

{Cyrus holds out his right pinky towards Curtis.}

CYRUS: Promise.

{Curtis agrees, but he was blind to the contents of this "promise". But he agreed, and locked pinkies with Cyrus.}

YOUNG CURTIS: What's your plan? How are you going to figure out who killed what's her name's mom? That girl?What's her name again?

CYRUS: Elizabeth? Yeah. But... the plan? I guess I'll just have to see in a few days from now. The only thing I really can do, is be there when it's supposed to happen.

{Before the conversation could continue, white lights from a truck pull into the driveway behind the Loans's car. Mr. and Mrs. Loans exit from the passenger side and the back seat. Who was driving the car could not be made out at this hour of nightfall.}

MR. LOANS: How'd the day go boys!?

{Mr. Loans hollered to Cyrus and Curtis sitting on the porch as he gathered his bearings.}

CURTIS: Just fine!

CYRUS: Just fine, Mr. Loans!

[4 Days later...]

{Cyrus stands rugged in his now overly worn white tee-shirt and signature black coat. Hand fiddling on the painkillers in his left coat pocket. Peering through the blinding sunlight down the long stretch of the upper middle-class community. The address Elizabeth

had given him before traveling into 2008 ahead of him. To be sure, he compared it to the folded strip of paper from his pocket. The land presented to each neighboring home was vast. Each home had brick columns on the left and right front ends of the driveway. The address of the homes were layered largely on the left brick of each home. Black mailboxes sat on the column as well. Cyrus looks to the watch on his left wrist to check the current time. 4:28 PM.}

CYRUS: I should have brought my shades.

{Cyrus starts to make his way down the block closer to the address. He gets a more vivid view of the home. Now, he can see that brick was the foundation of this home. The glare from the porch was from the screen door which had a white frame. The flattering red brick foundation was topped by a charcoal-colored roof. The closer Cyrus got, he could now see the dark brown front door behind the front door's screen. The wind blowing the stature of Cyrus in various directions. Cyrus checks his watch again... 4:31 PM. The nerves build as Cyrus takes a huge breath inward, then a huge outward breath. He now stands southwest of the home near the professionally crafted lawn of the neighbors. The grass of the neighbors, home green, and bushes along the bottom of the outstretched wing of the home where a horizontal window was tinted above the bushes. This is when Cyrus realized something looking over at the tinted window. His eyes squinted. This time, not because of the radiation of the

sun, but in utter confusion. He then thought back to 4 nights ago when he had pulled into the Loans driveway. It was February. Why had there been "vibrant bushes"? He thought back even more; his nerves rising as his lips were still with a slight opening. There had been beautiful weather the day he arrived. The weather of late spring. The weather had inconsistencies of any February he had known around Double-City. Blossoming trees and bushes in segments. He begins to fiddle more swiftly with the lid of the painkiller capsule in his left pocket. He turns back to the home of his focus. Checks his watch again... 4:35 PM. Just then, Cyrus starts to second guess himself just slightly. But not enough to make himself feel as though he were out of place. He was still prepared to enter that home. He watches his watch until the time reads 4:36 PM. Before he looks back up, instinct takes his eyes. There was a flash of white light from the left outstretched window of the home. Soon after, the front door slowly opens behind the screen, but no one's there. He waits to see if someone would appear, but no one does. The door just stays agate. He could not see beyond the screen to see any contents, but he could see there was no one coming out. Cyrus looks on as his adrenaline builds as he then rushes to the driveway with just a quicker paced walk. He stands at the end of the driveway and checks his watch again... 4:37 PM.

Cyrus walks through the front door. Holding the screen door so it does not bungee back to create noise. No lights were on. Where could that flash have come from? There was a large running Mayan designed rug. Velvet. Running over the dark laminated wooden lobby hallway. To the right of the rug from the view of the lobby, was a large staircase with a rail that had a circular bend clockwise on the right end of the staircase as the design from the view of the top of the stairs. Cyrus looked ahead to the left where there was a room. A room with seemingly large windows. The light from the outside glowed over the light grey carpet in that room. There was silence from that direction. Cyrus walks towards that room. In the room, there was a sitting area where a dark brown coffee table sat at the center, surrounded by various seating options which were leather and dark brown in synchrony. This had been the room where the flashing light had come from. But there was nothing there to cause such a flash. Not a person, or object. There had been a noise coming from the... "kitchen"? But not of endangering concern to the right of Cyrus past the dining room. He could stretch his neck slightly left to see the polished flooring. It sounded as though there was cleaning happening. Cyrus quickly looks around, and hides behind an outstretched wall to the left of the entrance from the hall's view where he entered. There was a large round clock above an end table fronting the center of the wall outing where Cyrus hid blocking off vision from the sitting area, dining room and kitchen. As Cyrus stood there, hoping and believing he would not be seen, he noticed a living area across from him surrounding a fireplace. He hears someone walk in from the other side of the wall, and hears what sounded like an unwrapping of a cord of some sort following. This cord was definitely attached to something. The folding of... no doubt this was... like *a vacuum. Cyrus peaks slowly around the corner to confirm. There was an elderly Hispanic maid with brunette, nearly red hair in a pink uniform preparing to vacuum the rug.}*

CYRUS: (The maid Elizabeth told me about.)

{The maid plugs in the vacuum on the wall closest to the open way leading to the dining room which was north of the kitchen. So her back was turned toward Cyrus. She up-pulls the vacuum's cording; being careful to not run it over when she flicks the vacuum switch to "on". The loud noise opens a window for Cyrus to slip back out of the room from the way he came in from the hallway. Creeping back to the front of the staircase as the hardwood floor under the rug made creaking sounds. Looking over his left shoulder to the 2nd level which was elongated horizontally with the master bedroom being presented with closed double doors that matched the wooden décor of the staircase and the floors in the center. Cyrus peers to the right where there had to be more bedrooms on the 2nd level of the house. Cyrus looked on to the stairs before climbing the staircase as quietly as he could. Careful not to creak the stairs; the sound was dimmed by the running vacuum. As soon as Cyrus reached the top, the floor was grey carpeting again. He peaked to the right where there were more doors. One having to be Elizabeth's room where she said she'd been painting her nails at this time. But the time had come. Cyrus walks quickly to the double doors, and grabs hold of

both door handles. Creaking sounds as he pushes forward through the door. Fully prepared. There was no time to think now. He had to go! It was 4:46 PM.

*As Cyrus goes through the doors, he sees a mattress with light blue blankets, and white sheets peeled backwards all disorganized-like. He looks straight ahead to see a man wearing a white t-shirt. He had a gelled 50s style hairdo, with strands hanging to his forehead. A woman lying on the bed, eyes completely shut. Cyrus then notices a bronze and brown dagger in her gut. Blood staining the gown she wore. The woman had dark hair, darker than Elizabeth's, but similar, and seemingly similar to Elizabeth in stature. Cyrus then looked on to the woman's face. She had similarities to Elizabeth, but certainly didn't look like a spitting image of her. She was still. She was dead. Cyrus then looks up to the man standing above the body. There was no resemblance. This was **certainly** not Elizabeth's father. The man then smiles at Cyrus. With the most intimidating smile he had ever seen. He had this "factor" about him. Like he **anticipated** this moment. He did not seem surprised at the site of Cyrus. Nor was he worried. There was water running to the left of Cyrus. A private restroom. There was a man showering behind the brown door. He knew because the man mumbled and hummed under the water, ridging his voice. **That** had to be Elizabeth's father. Cyrus knew it. He looked back over to the man. Still holding the downward grin. Cyrus was frozen with fear, yet curious. It was **this** man. **He** killed Elizabeth's mother. The Man folds his right elbow into his hip, and his palm to the sky. Blood* stained on them. He speaks to Cyrus. His voice creaked like the stairs, and was slightly deep.}

THE MAN: Oohh. This is too bad for you.

{*Cyrus's eyes then squint at the corners. Trying to narrow the predicament into purer understanding. Before Cyrus could make another thought, The Man* **vanished**. *Through a plasma of light very similar to the light Cyrus traveled through to make it to the year 2008 in. The Man was gone, and Cyrus was left with the lifeless mother of Elizabeth.*

Cyrus then hears the sounding of dim sirens. There was no doubt, it was the police. The sirens progressed and the shower shuts off in the restroom. Cyrus needed to decide what to do next with the situation unraveling right before his very eyes... Cyrus turns and runs back out of the room and down the staircase as quickly as he could. Eyeing each step on the way careful not to fall, being unfamiliar with the stairs. Creaking was still an issue, but it was not as big of a concern as being seen! The maid's vacuum shuts off. Now allowing the last two steps of the stairs to sound above the silence. As Cyrus makes it to the front screen door, he hears a young voice from up above behind him. It was Elizabeth's voice, and he knew it was. It made Cyrus's heart pound even faster. It caused a stall in his motion to escape. As he looked beyond the screen door into the street, 3 police squad cars were lined with lights flashing.}

YOUNG ELIZABETH: Nana!? What's going on!?

CYRUS: (Nana must be the maid.)

{*Cyrus thought swiftly. She **had** to be on her way into the hallway. No doubt. She would be walking into the hallway to see Cyrus in the lobby soon. Cyrus was at a loss of options. Cyrus pulls the handle, and busts through the screen door causing it to rapidly spring back quickly on its own. Cyrus stood on the porch, eyes on the police who are now quickly exiting their squad cars. Guns out. Cyrus had **one** calling card now.*}

CYRUS: PAUSE!

{*Nothing happened.*}

CYRUS: No, no, no. Fuck! (I'm still out of juice.) PAUSE! REWIND!

{*Nothing.*}

POLICE OFFICERS: FREEZE! PUT YOUR *GOD* DAMN HANDS UP!

{*Cyrus lifts his hands to the sky. There was no way out of this.*}

CYRUS S1C8:
IMPRISONED PAIN

NEWS REPORTER: It has been reported... that a young man was arrested today for breaking and entering, and murdering a woman in her sleep in Suburban Lake. Reports say the man entered the home with intentions currently unknown. The suspect has not been identified and is currently not cooperating with law officials.

{*Cyrus is walked down the corridor of the police station handcuffed with 4 officers trailing him. An officer to the left of him gripping his right elbow from behind. This officer was at least 6'4", 300lbs with a huge mustache, a bald fade haircut with spikes up top made with hair gel. He was well groomed. He is walked down to the interrogation room and sat down at the silver table. The table gave a strong metallic aroma that was bothersome. The officer began asking Cyrus questions before the interrogation phase started.*}

POLICE OFFICER: Want a drink while you wait?

CYRUS: No, thank you.

POLICE OFFICER: ... Anything I can get you?... Wanna make a phone call?

CYRUS: ... Sure.

{*Cyrus makes his phone call to the only people he could call. The Loanses.*}

MR. LOANS: Hello?

CYRUS: Hey! Can you hear me? It's... "Cyrus". I'm down at the police station. I got arrested—but it's not what you think. I didn't do anything.

You happen to caught the news?

MR LOANS: Yeah, this morning. What's going on?

{*Mr. Loans spoke as though he were completely clueless and unassuming, because he did not want to assume Cyrus's outrageous plan backfired. Also, both chose their words wisely careful that the line was wired and tapped.*}

CYRUS: You know the woman from Suburban Lake?

MR. LOANS: What woman?

CYRUS: The... one in Suburban Lake? The one that got killed?

{*Cyrus covers his mouth to whisper into the phone.*}

CYRUS: It's the woman I came here to save. Well, they think I did it.

MR. LOANS: Jesus Christ, Cyrus! Wha'—why? Just sit tight, and I'll have my lawyer down there. Now don't say anything until she gets there. Got it?

CYRUS: Yeah, I got it. Guessing... this is all over the news?

{*Mr. Loans took a moment to respond. Usually witty and quick to offend Cyrus, but he took his time to not make matters worse.*}

MR. LOANS: I was... in the kitchen with Curt' this morning, but I had the television on in the living room.

You know how talkative Curtis gets, but I've heard already. But don't worry! You just sit tight; we're gonna get this cleared up, okay?

CYRUS: Thanks.

MR. LOANS: Now you know not to answer any questions, right? Wait on the lawyer.

{Those words brought back another swift flashback of the lawful interrogation when he was a 16-year-old teenager. But he quickly snaps back to give an answer to Mr. Loans.}

CYRUS: Yeah. Yeah, I know. I won't. Thanks.

MR. LOANS: No problem, Cyrus! You just sit tight, okay?

CYRUS: Yes. Alright... bye.

{Cyrus neglected to inform Mr. Loans of the painkillers they found on him that did not seem legitimately issued due to the fact the year "2017" was not real yet. He is sat back down in the interrogation room. The lawyer arrives and sits down with Cyrus and the interrogator. The interrogator appeared to be younger.}

Only about 32 years old and clean shaved with a nice brown suit and black hair up top. A casual comb-over hairdo. A bit tacky for Cyrus's taste, but understandable fashion choices.}

INTERROGATOR: Hello. My name is Detective Shones, and I'll be handling this case for the moment.

{All of the officers there were so polite. Almost like they were simply taking care of their civil duties and neglecting anything in-between.}

DETECTIVE SHONES: So let me see...

{Shones whispers to himself as he looks through what the officers had provided him on the case in the files he had in front of him. Peeling back the manila folders uncovering a short stack of printed and inked white pages.}

DETECTIVE SHONES: So, why did you refuse to comply with the officers and reveal your identity?

CYRUS: I... —

CYRUS'S LAWYER: Ahmm.

{*The Lawyer gives an intentional attentive cough to attract the room's attention.*}

CYRUS'S LAWYER: Hello, my name is "Theresa Jackson". I'll be representing...

{*Theresa was in her 40s and wore a church purple suit. Flashy. She had golden hair of the red and orange spectrum. When she came into the room, her words to Cyrus were...*}

THERESA JACKSON: Hey how are you doin'? "Cyrus" is it?

{*Cyrus had forgotten to mention to Mr. Loans to not give his name away. But it could not be helped. Mr. Loans had to give all the information he could to the lawyer in order for her to help him.*}

CYRUS: Yes, but don't tell them that.

THERESA JACKSON: Oh don't worry, dear. They have nothing on you, so they have no right to know your name right now.

{*This is 2008, so "Stop-and-Identify" wasn't a lawful*}

tactic. This is also Double-City. "Stop-and-Identity" still isn't a valid form of law enforcement.}

THERESA JACKSON: ... my "Client".

DETECTIVE SHONES: Is there any reason your "Client" won't comply and reveal his identity?

THERESA JACKSON: Well because you all had no reason to assume him the murderer of this woman.

DETECTIVE SHONES: Yeah but what about...

{Detective Shones looked back down at his notes to comfort Theresa even though he knew the precision of his next exclamation...}

DETECTIVE SHONES: "Drug Possession" and "Breaking and Entering"?

THERESA JACKSON: Aside from the fact that you found prescribed drugs on my client with an invalid search reasoning, nor have you identified a proper timeline for the murder of this woman and my client's appearance on the scene, you have no conclusive evidence that he was not simply in the home trying to save this woman's life. Do you?

{*Shones takes a deep breath before answering. His personality now peeling back its covering. Thinly brash, yet calmly respectful and experienced. He had a certain arrogance that lined images of all of his years on the force. Showing those years in service were useful and warranted.*}

SHONES: Well, if your "Client" doesn't fess up now, it's going to be pretty hard to take back and back track the fact that he refuses to identify himself with officers of the law and broke into someone's home regardless of the reasoning. If everything goes well for him, the "Drug Possession" gets tossed out and he still sees some time behind bars.

{*That's how this part of the story concludes. 2 months after Cyrus was held without bail, he was sentenced to 3 **more** months behind bars with a $25,000 bail. The judge and jury could not find reason to not give Cyrus time, but they also had no reason to **convict** Cyrus of **more** time at this time. The problem was Cyrus had no fingerprints at the scene of the crime, and no motive to kill this woman. When they ran Cyrus's fingerprints, then later discovered they inevitably belonged to those of a 13-year-old boy, obviously there was a "Wtf?" response from the officers when they noticed the uncanny identical faces of both "Adult Cyrus" and "Kid Cyrus".*}

'Kid Cyrus' was trailed **to** and **from** school without the knowledge of the O'Brians where law enforcement

continued to try to match and make sense of the inves-
tigation. But what more could they have done? They
tried Cyrus for identity theft, but the two backgrounds
& personnel were 1-&-the-same of he and the kid!
This was not identity theft. Leak the story? Leak the
story. The story spread like a game of telephone with
well attentive students who all got straight "A"s by a
drunk on the force by the name of "Sebastian Kerry".
A lowdown dirty skeeze who got his kicks from lowly
drug dealers providing him with all kinds of narcot-
ics. How Sebastian functioned? No one knew with all
the shit he had in his system. Journalism stations paid
him $6,000 each on the side for the story.}

SEBASTIAN KERRY: You know that guy that killed that
woman in Suburban Lake? For no reason at all. Broke
into her home? Yeah, that guy like... must've—like...
time traveled or somethin'. He looks just like and has
the same fingerprints as some kid up in Base Park! Can't
be his father either. Father was located. Maybe a distant
relative who stole this kid's identity? Who knows! But
time travel sells. Again, he looks just like em'!

{*Sebastian was arrested on bribery, conspiring with*
confidential police evidence, extortion, blackmail, and
illegal substance possession charges.}

{*Theresa could not get Cyrus off on the drug possession*
charge. The doctor that prescribed the drugs, had not
prescribed them yet. This led to the denial of Cyrus's

bail 2 months in. *The court could not decide whether or not Cyrus was an endangerment to society and himself being in possession of drugs issued in the non-existent year of "2017". This **also** led to an investigation of a law student who had **no clue** who Cyrus was! He'd only practiced medicine for a year abroad before changing his mastery into law. Ultimately to later return to medicine in the year 2010. This was an act of God for him. The Judge conclusively theorized that Cyrus used the student as a ploy to gain access to unsolicited narcotics from an "unidentified foreign source".*

*Theresa was **also** unable to negate the fact that Cyrus broke into the home. Though with reason or without, it was **still** "Breaking-and-Entering".*

*In a month's time, this had become the biggest case in America. Also in Japan and China, and parts of Europe. **"IS TIME TRAVEL POSSIBLE?", "¿Es posible viajar en el tiempo?", "shí jiān lǚ xíng shì kě néng de ma?", "Le voyage dans le temps est-il possible?", "time travel wa kanou desu ka?"***

*{As Cyrus sat in prison for 2 months in his orange jumpsuit, the investigation continued on the outside by Elizabeth's family to convict Cyrus of the heinous crime. Mr. Wilson even threatened to have the multitude of charges escalated to the federal courts. With identity theft and terrorism still lingering, a much more **severe** sentencing was the only resolution for some. Like the*

Wilsons and O'Brians. The O'Brians pestered the Base Park Police (BPP) **constantly** *in that 2nd month for civil action. The confines of their son and the family's privacy had been compromised. Include the fact that the story had now carved such a pop culture following, it was not so difficult for the courts to, at the very* **least**, *ponder the case for supreme ruling.*

Several days into April, Cyrus was disturbed in his cell, lying on his cot by a guarding officer.}

GUARDING OFFICER: Hey, O'Brian, you got a visitor.

{Cyrus was walked down to the prison's parloir where he was expecting the Loans Family to come through the visitation doors. Cyrus sat at the silver table where that aroma began to smell again from the metal. Cyrus sat in a jail cell alone in his thoughts for an entire 2 months. Distraught from what had occurred. Now, sitting at that table waiting for the Loans Family. Having those same negative thoughts.}

CYRUS: Fuck!

{Cyrus mumbles to himself with blatant negativity.

As Cyrus sat in his own regrets concerned about what

*will happen to his friends, the timeline, and ultimately himself, tears began to slowly trickle down his face as he tries to hide them from all the other cellmates and visitors in the room. Some of them seemed to be having a decent time even though their loved ones were imprisoned. Some to never see the light of day, or dawn of night again. Never to have another drink with; to dine in a nice restaurant. But Cyrus's thoughts just kept going back to **her**. How he failed **her**. Will he ever see **her** again? Even worse, even if he **does** make it back to his time, does this mean he would never meet Elizabeth and fall in love with her? This time, Cyrus had no painkillers to help pass the time.*

As he sat there looking into the metal surface of the appalling table observing the tears as they landed, he hears the door above open so loudly it could wake God himself from a slumber. Cyrus looks up, and there he was coming through the door casually. The man that murdered Elizabeth's mother.}

CYRUS S1C9: IGOR HANNICK

{Cyrus's pupils dilating as tears are still evident along his cheeks and form a crescent in his eyes. The Man across from him still wore his white t-shirt, and his hair still smoothly greased as he walked towards Cyrus with a grin so sinister, it could rile up a nun. As he walks with his chin lowered, he had very little facial hair surrounding his pointed masculine features.

Bubbles shroud the interior of Cyrus's belly. As the man gets closer and closer, the bubbles in Cyrus's belly begin to rise and rise until they reach his forehead creating a steam that causes him to leap from his steal seat in a faceless rage.}

CYRUS: YOU!! YOU MOTHERFUCKER!!! YOU DID THIS!!! I'M GOING TO KILL YOU—...

{Before he could continue on his tirade, guarding officers rush over to contain him at his bonded core. Arms flailing above the shoulders of the officers. He

continues to unravel an almost aimless rage.}

CYRUS: HE... DID IT!!! HE KILLED HER!!! LET ME GO!!! YOU MOTHERFUCKER!!!

OFFICERS: STOP! STOP!... STOP NOW!... GET HIM OUT OF HERE!

THE MAN: Please, please let him go! I have something very important to tell him. Do not take him away!

{Cyrus's rage begins to calm as he hears the man speak. Unconsciously, he wanted to know more about the man who'd framed him for murder. The death of the mother of the woman he loves. Cyrus's vision clears as he had seen only blackness as he scrambled to be free of the officers containing him.}

OFFICERS: SIR, will you calm down!?

CYRUS: Alright, alright.

OFFICERS: What's going on here!?—

THE MAN: Nothing, nothing! Please, let him stay here!

{*He stops squirming to see the eyes of The Man. Shadowed by the darkness of the lower and upper lids of the eye. They were the color of dark gravel on a rainy day. At least they appeared so to Cyrus. The Man motions his right hand towards the table before he sits himself down across from the shambled Cyrus suggesting Cyrus have a seat with him. He had a mannerism that was unlike anything Cyrus had ever seen. He was growing more curious of this stranger. He sits down as the bubbles begin to flow back down to his belly.*}

OFFICERS: Not another outburst like that! You good?

CYRUS: ... Yes.

{*Officers back away and begin to return to their posts.*}

OFFICER: Fuckin' punk.

{*Cyrus feels an uneasiness on his exterior before he starts to question The Man with a cringed tone.*}

CYRUS: Who the fuck are you? Why'd you do it? Don't fucking lie to me!

THE MAN: My name is "Igor Hannick".

{Cyrus was undoubtedly expecting deflection. It did not happen.}

IGOR HANNICK: So you're Cyrus? Right in front of me. I thought you'd be... well, you're exactly what I thought you'd be; frail, fragile, young and naive. A fool. Stupid. Just foolish. But! Don't get yourself too worked up again, because you should probably hear what I have to say to you. And then you can get as worked up as you want. But don't go overboard, because I'm posting your bail.

{Cyrus is now utterly fazed by the cockiness and ill-equipped persona of this man "Igor Hannick". He could hardly make out the situation. Posting his bail? His face wore a grim disgust he could not alter at the moment due to his inner lack of comfortability. He could only whisper pitifully. Completely broken by this "Igor Hannick".}

CYRUS: What the fuck are you? What are you—posting my bail.—

IGOR HANNICK: Don't you worry! I'm goin' to get you out of here. I'm going to confess to the murder in front of the entire world. I'm just thinking of the production, and how I'm going to put it on. With the technology you guys have in this time, ahh, I'm going to be famous. Isn't that right?

CYRUS: You... you can time jump.

IGOR HANNICK: Well of course I can! Which of us can't? Ahehe —

CYRUS: ("Us"? Who is "us"? I need as much information as possible. One question at a time.) You're fucking sick. Why did you do it? You still haven't answered my question. And how can you time travel? Posting my bail? You feel guilty.

{*Igor Hannick gives off a smile to the sky like he was thinking of something as sweet as the lips of a woman he had kissed.*}

IGOR HANNICK: Ahh, no reason—no guilt. I just want you to be as miserable as possible. Right before I kill you, you know? I figured it'd be more entertaining that way. And your second question, I was blessed with it. Just like you.

(*Cyrus's eyes widen as the bubbles start to rise back up. Now tightening his chest causing his eyes to bulge in terror. Trying not to make it obvious to Igor that he was terrified out of his mind.)*

CYRUS: ...Why? —

IGOR HANNICK: "Why", "Why", "why", "why"—is that all you can say?

I haven't figured out how I want to kill you yet, okay? .... Do I want to slit your throat? Do I want to... shoot you in the head and have all of your brains everywhere—maybe too messy. Suffocation is a lot cleaner. I've already stabbed someone in the gut so... that's out of the question—

CYRUS: You mentioned, *"Technology"—our* "technology". Where are you from? What time?

IGOR HANNICK: ... I don't think you know how any of this works, and I really don't feel the need to explain this to you because you'll be dead. Shortly.

CYRUS: Why do you want me dead? What'd I ever do to you?

{*Igor looks closer into the eyes of Cyrus. Observing.*}

IGOR HANNICK: Are you crying? Of course you are! Fucking despicable. What a fucking faggot!

*{Some of the guests in the room that **heard** Igor, instantly trigger in offence at the sound of the "F" word. Yet no one vocally expresses their dissatisfaction to Igor.}*

IGOR HANNICK: I can't *wait* to punch you in that *goofy* little face of yours!

CYRUS: Why?—(God, I just asked, "Why?" Again.)

IGOR HANNICK: "Why", "Why", "Why"; there's that word again. You *exist*. That's why I want you dead. That way, I can claim your power. You know, like "*villains*" do?

CYRUS: (We're getting somewhere.) You mean, "steal" my power. How?

IGOR HANNICK: Ehh, give or take. "Potato", "Potahto". "Tomato", "Tomahto". But it's more of a "*claim*". Any-who...

{Igor gives an un-convincing look down at his watch as he prepares to get up from his seat. Uncrossing his

left foot from over his right knee. But Cyrus had more questions & comments. Attempting to entice Igor to continue the conversation.}

CYRUS: Well I... I hate to break it to ya', but my power's gone.

IGOR HANNICK: ... Ahahaha, your powers aren't "gone", you idiot. You just can't access them right now.

{Igor is now moved by Cyrus's ignorance. So he stays around for more conversation. Leaning onto the table forearms down. Tilting his head towards Cyrus as though he was letting Cyrus in on a secret. As much as Cyrus despised Igor from his first and second encounters, he could not deny how incredibly good-looking he was.}

IGOR HANNICK: ... This is the part where the "*antagonist*" gives the "*protagonist*" a slither of hope by filling him in on how he can get out of said predicament, but not this story. This is *my* story! And... you have to die. Now if you excuse me, I have a very important place to be. The show *must* go on!...

{Igor looks back down on his watch. This time, it was sincere. Then, he starts to turn to leave Cyrus there puddled in his own confusion.}

IGOR HANNICK: I have a press conference to crash. I have to let the people know that it was me who killed that woman. Whatever her fucking name was.

{Igor gets up and walks away from the table with his head held high. causing a swift breeze to brush under Cyrus's nose. Cyrus's head rises slightly with confidence.}

CYRUS: Her name was "Sonya", you *fucking* prick!

{Igor is unfazed by the insult as he continues to walk with his head held high, and notions the back of his right index, middle, and thumb fingers up as to say "good-bye" to Cyrus as he walks through the incredibly thundering doorway again. Cyrus knew there was no way the officers would believe this "Igor Hannick" had just confessed to the murder of Sonya Wilson. So he stayed quiet. Resenting his defeat.}

IGOR HANNICK: Whatever.

{A short two hours later, Cyrus was released on bond. Wearing his plain not-so-white tee shirt again. Holding his black coat over his right forearm. He trudges as quickly as he can towards the lobby of the prison. His adrenaline now pacing back and forth, up and down his being. He was temporarily free. Yet, feeling he

*was seemingly walking towards his very own death. Thinking of every word this "Igor Hannick" had expressed to him. He was true to his word in bailing him out, he murdered Sonya Wilson... he **clearly** had no trouble murdering.*

As he passes the outer windowed automated doors separating the holding side of the prison campus from the entry side of the campus, he looks up to the right of him and sees the outdated 1990s television up high in the corner of the lobby. His hearts sank to his stomach as he starts to feel sweat seep from his pores.}

NEWS REPORTER: We're here at the scene where just over an hour ago, several bombs went off in front of the Double-City Northwestern Suburban Lake City Hall right before—a man who says his name is *"Igor Hannick"*, walked up to the podium of the monthly press conference held here—*screaming*—**yelling** at press to continue filming with various violent threats, they say—as the man claimed to be the killer of the woman in the county over just 2 *months* ago. Several officers were injured in the incident on and around the podium. Officers have attempted to tail the suspect out to an abandoned gas station—as we have our sky crew following the chase further out west of Northwestern County. Officers have *not* apprehended, *or attempted* to approach the car—the gas station, excuse me, as they suspect to be met with deadly force. Names of the officers injured in today's tragedy have not yet been released to the public at this time.

CYRUS S1C10: THE STORY OF THE DIM ROSE

[Days before the murder of Mrs. Wilson...]

{The Young Elizabeth Wilson attends the neighborhood middle school, Suburban Lake Middle. She wore something of a uniform, though it was not required. A corduroy, overall skirt with buttons over a browning white sweater. Her days were often a mystery being in-between social classes. She didn't have enough relationships that caused a Saturday or Sunday morning to be contrived with exhaustion after enjoyment. Yet un-lame enough to decide the outcome of her days based on a particular emotion she felt of a single day. Her best friend's name was Chyna Sue. But she did not see her regularly. Only on her lunch and free period. And after school.

*The crossover into middle school from Elementary school is **always** a game of Tetris. How ever the blocks fall, the game will go on until too many pieces were out of place. Causing a tragic ending in the* *description of bad rumors and outright fist fights. But if the pieces **did** fall into place, life goes on as it did in Suburban Lake Elementary School. The reward was mildly sweet at times, but not everlasting. Who could possibly remember a game of Tetris they've won?*

Chyna Sue was the only kid who did not care how Elizabeth dressed in contradiction to how much money her family made. So after school, they'd wait for their after-school-pick-up on the side of the curb where parents could drop-off and pick-up students. Two peas in a pod.}

CHYNA SUE: So do you want to hang out this weekend? My parents said I can come over if Mr. & Mrs. Wilson aren't tired of me.

YOUNG ELIZABETH: Nooo, my parents never get tired of you! I think they like you more than they like me.

CHYNA SUE: Hahaha, nooo that's not true. We're pretty much the same; I'm just the Asian version of you.

{They both laugh; the key to the longevity of their friendship.}

CHYNA SUE: Mrs. Wilson is picking you up today, right? I'll just ask her myself.

{Elizabeth did not respond. Seeming displeased in some manner.

Chyna's mother arrives in her crème, grey & blue freshly washed car. Rolls down the window, and motions for Chyna to get in. The girls catch eye of Mrs. Sue and finish their endless compliments to one another.}

CHYNA SUE: Liz', your mom is awesome.

{Chyna stands up and sprints to the passenger's side of the car. Her bright pink backpack popping up and down with every step. Causing all the school supplies inside to create a synchronized calamity. A wondrous sound to some, because no matter how much commotion the sound caused, the owner of the backpack never stopped running. Or maybe they just never figured out how to stop the bouncing school supplies. The sound was treacherous to others. Especially the students who could not afford as many school supplies, or to the other adolescent students who felt the child was above the age of such eagerness for life, or the students who were always the last to be picked up from the school stoop.}

CHYNA SUE: I'll call you!

{*Chyna yelled back to Elizabeth as she got in the car.*}

CHYNA'S MOTHER: LIZ'!? LIZ, did you want a ride or your mother's close by on her way?

ELIZABETH: No thanks, Mrs. Ann. My Mother will be here soon; she's not too far away!

MRS. ANN: Okay, sweetheart.

{*Mrs. Ann turns her head and drives off.*

15 minutes later, at 3:05 PM, Mrs. Wilson arrives in her white 2008 minivan. Rolls down the window talking on her flip-phone. She interrupts her own conversation to yell out through the passenger's side.}

MRS. WILSON: Come on, Elizabeth!

{*Liz gets up and walks towards the van with her head slightly low. Looking at her mom continue her phone conversation with her auburn shades sitting on top of her head holding her beautiful blonde hair back. Liz gets in. Mrs. Wilson again interrupts her phone conversation to take a second to give Liz some affection.*}

MRS. WILSON: Honey, I thought I told you to stop wearing those clothes. —

{*And then she goes back to her phone conversation before pulling off of the school lot.*}

MRS. WILSON: Yes... Yes... you tell them 'Sonya Deanne Wilson' will not put up with anymore of the nonsense! You're in an all-women's club, dress like it. No jeans! No tennis shoes! I don't get what's so hard to understand.—what's so hard to understand!?

{*Elizabeth looks down at her appearance in conjunction with the statements her mother made about women in her Women's Club. The direct statement about her clothes did not break confidence, it was the statements made about the other women. This could be what Sonya thought of Elizabeth but never said. Elizabeth looks back to her mother's clothes which showed enough cleavage to cause lust upon her beautiful chest. Yet showed little enough to be considered upper-class classy. Her right wrist jangled with a large golden bracelet, and a huge golden & diamond ring on her right index finger as she navigated the car all the way to their home. The only other words Sonya spoke to Liz on the way home was...*}

SONYA WILSON: Be sure to change when we get home—we have a dinner to go to for your dad.

{Elizabeth took those words in favor, because she could spend time with her mother and father. She was her father's pride and joy. A blooming white lotus in a dying field that had daily rain and no sun.

Sonya pulls into the driveway and quickly exits the car where you could now see the entire layout of her captivating black outfit. Decorated with gold and high heels clucking up the driveway as she comes to the abrupt end of her phone conversation.}

SONYA: Yes, I'll talk to you later, sweetie. Okay bye.

{The lingering New York City accent sounded like the harp she heard down the hall in her 5th period Geometry Class. She could never play a harp or violin. Sonya would never allow it. So, she admired the lucrative motions of vibration from afar.

Sonya shuts her phone and walks through the front door as she called to her husband.}

SONYA: Steve!? Steve—sweetie we're here!

{From the kitchen wearing a suit older than Elizabeth herself came her father. He was in his forties having short dark grey and brown hair like a porcupine. He stood 3 to 4 inches taller than Sonya who was 5 feet 8 inches tall, and had an uncanny resemblance to Elizabeth.}

SONYA: God, honey—why are you so orange?

STEVE WILSON: I was in the backyard this morning.

{Steve opens his arms revealing his chest and his belly which showed he had been a father for some time. Embracing Sonya as only a father or husband could. Sonya stops before embracing Steve to whiff a disgusted, instinctive snarl at him.}

SONYA: You wearing that?

{Steve looks down holding his palms upward in offence to the comment. Is she saying what he wore was not presentable enough for her? Steve longed to always please Sonya. So, he always showed the ruffles along the edges of his eyes and presented his teeth.}

STEVE: Yeah?—What's wrong with it?

{*Sonya now had this disgusted sarcastic smug reaction.*}

SONYA: Nothin' much.—

Honey—Liz, go change.

{*A twelve-year-old child seeing their parents exchanging truths, exposing teeth and red cheeks is a joy every child wished to have as a reality. And it was Elizabeth's reality. What more could she have asked for? And the exposed teeth and red cheeks of her father alone was enough for her to feel she lived in a castle in the highest of far away and protected lands with every want she could ever request.*}

SONYA: You're not wearing that! God—I swear, you and your daughter... she gets this from you! You're like twins! Two peas in a pod.

{*Elizabeth turned and rushed up the stairwell.*}

{*7 o'clock rolls upon the day. The Wilson family arrives at an Italian 5 Star restaurant no one could possibly pronounce.*}

GREETER: Good Evening, did the family have reservations?

STEVE: Yes, we're here for the 'Barry's Benefit Banquet'.

GREETER: Alright, right this way.

{*The Greeter was a young Romanian male who wore a black tuxedo which stood to accent the freshly plucked and opened grapefruit walls trimmed with gold. Through the arch centered in the restaurant separating the reserved seating from the party reserved venue side was a room full of jewelry laced bodies reflecting the lights on the walls and ceiling. Sonya stood at the hip of Steve grasping the sleeve of the expensive all cotton caramel colored pea coat he wore. She observed all of the images portrayed in each conversation across the room.*}

STEVE: Ah, there's Mr. Barry over there.

{*Mr. Barry had a white mane fit for a CEO, with a face radiant and orange. His wife wore a black bedazzled dress made of real diamonds with a diamond bracelet and crystal shaped earrings to match. Her mid-length blonde hair made her look elegant. A Queen fit for a King in their empire casting wisdom to anyone who'd seek it.*}

STEVE: Mr. Barry how are you, sir?

MR. BARRY: Steve! Hey how's it goin'?

{*As Steve approached the Barry's with his wife still holding onto him, she observed the room trying to make sense of where she would possibly be able to fit into the mold of the environment. Seeing so many well-kept women in their latest edition, one-of-a-kind dresses and 'end of the line' jewelry.*}

MR. BARRY: This must be your wife! And ... is that your daughter!?

STEVE: Ah, yes this is my wife, "Sonya"...

SONYA: Hi how are ya'?

STEVE: And my beautiful daughter, "Elizabeth."—Say "hello" Elizabeth.

ELIZABETH: Hi.

{*Elizabeth was just 12 years old, but felt more at ease in the presence of her father in that restaurant than her mother did. There were other children in the room Liz's age. She scoured and felt the urge to acquaint herself with her peers wearing her red dress that her mother handpicked for her whilst on a 'Girls Day Out' Saturday shopping spree. Sonya thought it was eloquent for her skin tone that had a much darker pigment than her own. Also, matching the brown straight locks Elizabeth wore. Bringing her green eyes to life.}*

MRS. BARRY: Very nice to meet you all... and your daughter, isn't she precious, Mark!?

MR. BARRY: Yes, honey.

How old is she?

SONYA: She's 12, and just going to Middle School.

MR. BARRY: Ahh, what school?

SONYA: She's going to Suburban Lake. —

MR. BARRY: "Suburban Lake"—that's the public school, right dear?

{Sonya had a displeasure in that rhetorical question under her false smile.}

MRS. BARRY: Yes, it is, dear.

MR. BARRY: You know, Steve, our grandson goes to Bridgeton. I can get you the info.

{Sonya became more and more displeased and felt a direct stabbing of her upbringing and how she was currently raising her daughter. Elizabeth knew her mother well as she looked up at her and felt and saw the distress she was under. Sonya deflected the conversing circle by searching the room once more. She soon noticed some of the women from her Women's Club, and decided to break free of her husband and the uneasiness she felt speaking with the Barry Family.}

SONYA: You know what, honey, I think I see some of my girls over there. I'm just gonna go say "hello" if you don't mind.

STEVE: Okay, honey.

{Sonya twisted towards Liz.}

SONYA: Stay with your father, okay sweetheart?

ELIZABETH: Okay, Mom.

{*Sonya broke free, and crouched as she approached her friends in her black high heels. Unfortunately, even in the black she wore, her room presence, height, blonde hair and large perfectly white smile always gave her away.*}

SONYA: Hi, Girls!

{*The women all greeted Mrs. Wilson with a smile and hello. They all had black or brown hair. Elizabeth's eyes followed every motion her mother made. The only blonde of the group. Elizabeth would never be able to make out what was being said in the group, but she noticed the constant preening of her mother.*}

{*Later that night when the Wilsons returned home, Elizabeth spent quality time with her father by their fireplace. Laughing and telling stories together. Having snacks and hot chocolate, wearing fitted comfort wear you could sleep in for days before the stench and realization that you'd been wearing those clothes to bed for days kicks in. By the end of it, Steve kissed his daughter on the forehead, and went off to bed. Except when he returned to his room, he found his*} *wife, Sonya, in the restroom sat in front of the large mirror above the handcrafted sink. She'd been gazing sharply at herself. Steve was stood up in one place looking over his left shoulder through the doorway of the bathroom from the center of the bedroom. Sockless, staring at his beautiful wife.}*

STEVE: Honey?

{He approached the restroom and leaned against the doorway. He was frozen before being careful not to let out an expression that would make his observation more uncomfortable with his openly concussed curiosity.}

STEVE: You dyed your hair?

{Something was clearly bothering Sonya as he glared at his wife's freshly wet brunette hair. She did not turn from her mirror.}

SONYA: ... I'm the only one in the family who's blonde...

{Sonya then turned to her husband with a false smile, but Steve knew the woman he'd loved for so long. Nothing could leave an emotional disparity like the sadness of his wife. In her hazel eyes was tears she'd

wiped before he entered the room and before he crept his way up the creaking staircase. Sonya wanted to be happy for her loving husband, but she felt she could not. She would pretend to be until it was true.}

SONYA: I figured I'd even things out a bit. Join the club.

{Sonya wanting to "even things out," made "things" odd, and her intertwining with joy and happiness for the love of her husband, the feeling that she belonged... never became true. Just 2 days later, Sonya Wilson, was murdered.}

CYRUS S1C11: A FOOD CHAIN

{*Cyrus calls Mr. Loans from the prison's Guest lobby. Mr. Loans was first to speak.*}

MR. LOANS: Hello? Cy'?... Is that you?

CYRUS: Yeah... I'm just waiting in the lobby.

MR. LOANS: How long have you been out?

CYRUS: Oh, don't worry. They just let me go—out, about... 10 minutes ago or so?

MR. LOANS: Alright, you stay put. I'm on my way, okay?

CYRUS: Okay.

{*Cyrus hangs up the phone and sits in the waiting area just under the television. Across from him, the gaoler had her curly hair tied back as she had both hands placed on papers of documentation moving her pen across them. They were the only two in the room. Cyrus watched her with numbing stillness on his face as he hears the daunting reports come from the television in the quality of streaming an online viral video in the lowest resolution quality possible. The officer never looked up. Cyrus felt... foggy. His immediate reaction was a focused house cat awaiting disturbing action from the human who deemed themselves in control because they held an item that would trigger the cat with little effort in the stalemate as she plucked the pen across the desk creating that popping and landing sound. Clutching onto his large black coat. Sitting without much movement as he then remembered the cold he felt sitting at the bus stop in the middle of a Double-City winter at 6:19 AM in the mornings awaiting the school bus that was always 4 minutes behind schedule.*}

CYRUS: (Does she not hear the TV?)

{*Mr. Loans arrived 15 minutes later. Cyrus got up and walked out of the front lobby's doors when he saw Mr. Loans pulling up to the front entrance. He had that feeling again; though he had felt the outside air on his face, he did not feel free. He felt he was walking towards his imminent death with the cold feeling from Igor Hannick still prevalent.*}

MR. LOANS: Cyrus!

{Cyrus got into the car, and they rode off.

Mr. Loans struggled to find words to comfort Cyrus. He had never seen him in this manner; completely broken. Snot stale above his upper lip. His eyes on the edge of descension.}

MR. LOANS: ... You doing okay?

CYRUS: ... I'm okay.

{Mr. Loans had so many questions, but couldn't figure out how to ask them without a snapping reaction. Hoping Cyrus would welcome him.}

MR. LOANS: Who's this guy that bailed you out?

{Nothing from Cyrus.}

MR. LOANS: Cyrus, what the hell is going on?

{Cyrus knew he could not withhold information

anymore. He was trapping himself in his own mental tracks.}

CYRUS: It was the guy. He... he...

{Cyrus felt the fear growing in his cheeks and eyes with every word. But he continued.}

CYRUS: He... murdered all those cops. It was *that* guy.

Mr. LOANS: What!?... Cyrus...

CYRUS: That *guy*. That *man*...

MR. LOANS: You mean that guy that damn near blew up the entire police department!? He's the one that bailed you out? *That* guy?

CYRUS: "Igor Hannick". his name is, "Igor Hannick".

{Mr. Loans is appalled, but not surprised by the murderous intentions of Igor Hannick since he'd heard the story earlier in the day from the newscasters. Though he was obviously surprised he was somehow intertwined with Cyrus's life.}

MR. LOANS: Yeah, I heard it on the news. My God, none of this makes any sense! Why would he bail you out after he murdered the woman and framed you for it? Then, he blew up the entire police department? What's this guy's deal? And why is he after you? This have something to do with what you can do? You know... —

CYRUS: He can do what I can do. Well, what I could do before. Powers are still gone. He... time jumped right in front of me when he killed Sonya Wilson.

MR. LOANS: *How?*—Why?—Why is he doing any of this? I don't understand. "Sonya Wilson." Is that the woman, right? How can he do what you can?

{*Cyrus now thinking back to the conversation he had with Igor as he continuously questioned "Why?" before he responded.*}

CYRUS: I don't know.

It's just a game. It's just a game for him.

{*Cyrus puts his head back hopelessly against the headrest as tears are flowing uncontrollably from his eyes now. All he could see was wavering water in his sight.*

Mr. Loans navigating the brisk road. High winds cradling the air with water flailing.}

MR. LOANS: You've... spoken with this guy before? You know him?

CYRUS: ... He came to visit me.

{Cyrus tilts his head to the left.}

CYRUS: A few hours ago.

{Cyrus was offended inside of himself that Mr. Loans would ask such a question of his familiarity with Igor Hannick.}

CYRUS: No... I don't know him. He just... came to visit me. I'd only seen him once before. When he murdered Sonya Wilson.

{This shocks Mr. Loans.}

MR. LOANS: Right before he blew up the damn police station? He was there? *He* killed her?

{*Mouthing and explaining this all to Mr. Loans was breaking him.*}

CYRUS: ... and he's gonna kill me next. What am I gonna do!? I'm going to die, I'm going to die, I'm going to die! —

MR. LOANS: What happened to your powers? —

CYRUS: They just vanished. He said they're locked away. But they're just gone, and I'm going to die! I'm going to die, man I'm going to... die —

MR. LOANS: Hey, hey, hey!

{*Mr. Loans interrupts Cyrus's loathing. Completely afraid of his next words. Yet knowing what he would say next would give Cyrus the life he needed.*}

MR. LOANS: Suck it up!

{*Mr. Loans kept his eyes forward, as he now granted his body feeling to speak from his heart.*}

MR. LOANS: I was a kid—when I was a kid, my father,

he would take me out to go hunting with him. We'd sit up in a tree for hours. Waiting for a deer to pop up and sit in range long enough for us to get a good shot of em'. I mean, I didn't do much shooting when I hunted with my dad. I didn't start shooting until a couple years later. But you know what he taught me? I asked, "Why do we sit up here so long waiting just to probably get one shot and *one* deer?" He told me, "We sit up here to get away from your mother." Ahahaha. And then he said, "Wouldn't you run if you knew someone was tryin' to hurt ya'? It's in their nature. They're afraid of humans, so they stay as far away as possible. That's why we only get '*one* shot at... *one* deer.' The only time they wonder out, is when they need to get food; provide for their families. We're the same way. We sense danger, we avoid it at all costs, right?" Haha, I said... "Yeah, Dad." Then he said, " We're at the top of the food chain, but if we step into *their* homes where *their* families are, the playing field is leveled *simply* based on the need for survival and protecting what they love. Doing whatever is necessary." So here's your lesson, Cyrus. Whose den has this man stepped in? Yours? Or his?

{*The stillness of the warm tears on Cyrus's face lay frozen on his red cheeks and did not flow further even though his head was held low to cause the tears to run. Waiting for them to fall. It did not happen. Mr. Loans now felt like he was taking care of his son. As Cyrus was to him. He comforted him with a suggestion unrelated to the current circumstance, but the words he chose would be cheerful in any situation.*}

MR. LOANS: Let's go get somethin' to eat then head back to the house. You hungry? Whatcha' in the mood for?

{*Deciding what "mood" you're in for dinner is always a daunting task. For Mr. Loans, he knew he would receive no suggestions from Cyrus. Cyrus was visibly on the corner of "accept defeat", or "fight for survival". It isn't any easier to decide what to have for dinner. The common American denominator is 'pizza'.*

The purr of the car's quiet engine is all that could be heard all the way to the lot of the local pizza joint, 'Toni's Pizza'. The place was built as a dine-in restaurant in the 1950s. Mucky from the disgruntled concrete on the parking lot, to the chipped white paint on the outside of the diner. The restaurant had been franchised all over Double-City, but this was the original. Before Mr. Loans stepped out of the car, he had another important question for Cyrus.}

MR. LOANS: Pepperoni or sausage?

CYRUS: Uhm... sausage. Thanks.

{*Mr. Loans hopped his way to the entrance. Cyrus stepped out of the car as well to seemingly get some fresh air. The wind continued to blow as he reached into his coat pocket once more. Searching for a sense of relief. He could not find it. So he stood there. Continuing to deliberate.}*

{Mr. Loans returned with a large sausage pizza in one hand. Fiddling for his keys in his pocket in the other.}

CYRUS: I help people grow and establish their businesses.

MR. LOANS: What's that?

{Mr. Loans squinted. He didn't make out the remark that well. Cyrus turned his face over his left shoulder to speak to Mr. Loans with more attention.}

CYRUS: That's my job. In the future, I help businesses grow. Help find investors. Give business and marketing ideas and strategies.

{At random; was Mr. Loans supposed to make something of these confessions?}

MR. LOANS: ... You sure you supposed to be telling me this stuff?

{Cyrus responded next with a smile.}

CYRUS: No. But what exactly *are* we sure of right now? I know, I've overcome a lot in my life. Things I can't tell you about.

MR. LOANS: ... seems like you've made your decision?

{Cyrus looks out to the sky before responding.}

CYRUS: ... I've helped so many people grow. I have these abilities, at least the Igor guy says I still do. There's gotta be a reason for all of this. For all of the money I've made, the ... things I've overcome, and the abilities I have. I have to know what that reasoning is. I have to know why.

{Mr. Loans stopped. Hunched over preparing to put his key into the car door with the large pizza held up in the other hand. Always forgetting he could just press a button on the key fob to open the damn door. His vision of the life Cyrus had grown for himself in the future became prevalent and appeasing. A slanted smile grew on his face. And a joy in his eyes he never really showed Curtis and Cyrus. Always prepared to teach, he could never show them how proud of a father he was outside of special occasions. They wouldn't take him seriously. They'd believe he were easy to please.

At this point, he recognized Cyrus as his superior. There was nothing more he could ever teach him.}

MR. LOANS: You're rich. In the future?

{Cyrus smiles back.}

MR. LOANS: That's my boy. Alright let's get back home and have some dinner. We can talk about how we gonna beat this guy.

{Cyrus smiled harder, and then got back into the car.}

CYRUS S1C12: THE NEWSROOM

{The spiced aroma of fresh Italian sausage, and the warm mist of the hot pizza filled the car. The conversation continued with Cyrus now showing signs of hope.}

MR. LOANS: So... what's so special about this girl? We've talked about why you've come this far. I trusted you, you didn't tell us much. Why?

{Cyrus peers over his left shoulder turning away from the cold window now fogged from the aroma from the pizza.}

CYRUS: What else is there to know?

{Mr. Loans peers over before giving a response.}

MR. LOANS: Cyrus O'Brian, I known you all yer life. You never done anything this nuts. You've traveled years and years back to stop some "murder" from happenin'. Always lookin' for somethin'. I really hope you couldn't also be looking for the music. The music on the radio is... you know we had the hip-hop back then, but...—

CYRUS: Oh, come on. It's not bad. 2008 was a... was a great year! 2013 was... a great year.

MR. LOANS: Okay, okay. Point being, any man going through all this trouble, a girl's involved, and she must be important. We know she's involved, and she must be really important.

{Cyrus let out a breath of sensibility with the looming difficulties floating in the car. The air in the car much lighter now than before. He turns to look through the windshield with a smirk. A small red blush forming in his cheeks much lower in vibrancy than the red glowing from the backlights of the car ahead of them as rain began to fall again dispersing the glow of the lights.}

MR. LOANS: So, answer the question. What's so special?

{Cyrus pillows the back of his skull into the head of the seat now with a wider smile on his face. Showing teeth.}

MR. LOANS: Come on now! The woman that got murdered, that's what you were trying to stop, right?

CYRUS: Yeah—I mean I've told you this much. —

MR. LOANS: I don't want you to revisit the scene. Definitely don't want you to do that. But I just would like ta' know why ya' come all this way for this girl. Putting yer own self at risk.

{Mr. Loans treading over the murder of Sonya Wilson politely.}

CYRUS: She's... she's... just special.

MR. LOANS: Okay, like how?

CYRUS: I can't really explain it, Mr. Loans. She makes me feel... like I can be something better, you know? Honestly, I wish I knew more about her.

MR. LOANS: Wait, so you don't really know this girl?
CYRUS: I do. I do. I know all the little things about her... no one knows. All the little things she does. Her knacks. The way she rubs her belly while she eats. She's like a boy in that matter.

MR. LOANS: Hm.

CYRUS: Yeah, you know how guys overstuff their face and lean back in their chair?

{Cyrus now warming up to idea of presenting the concept of Elizabeth Wilson to Mr. Loans with a huge vulnerable smile.}

CYRUS: She ruffles her nose when she smiles—more than the average. Yet she's still listening through the laughter. She's, so cute. She's... sensitive. I've honestly never really seen her get angry with anyone. She's understanding. People may see her and think she's ordinary, but to me, she's peace. Doing this is me showing her and not just telling her how I feel. Ya' know?

{Mr. Loans keeps his left hand on the wheel, and his eyes forward listening and interpreting the situation under his own will.}

MR. LOANS: How did you meet this girl?

{Cyrus puts on a stern mask.}

MR. LOANS: Right. —

CYRUS: We met... over 2 years ago in my time. —

MR. LOANS: And you're like, what, 23? 24?

{*Cyrus polishes his mask.*}

MR. LOANS: Okay, okay.

{*Cyrus uncovered more of his truth. vividly dreaming of the moment he met Elizabeth through sparkles and beautiful diamonds.*}

CYRUS: She never even noticed me at the time. It took me two entire months to gather up the courage to finally speak to her. And when I finally did, she was as gentle as what I envisioned her to be.

I'd watch her walking from up in my office passing below on the street. Every day she'd... look so beautiful. Always presentable—like she had to present the biggest pitch to a room full of Double-City heavyweights. When we spoke for the first time it was... okay. After that, we'd exchange passing looks for another month when we came across each other downtown. Until we spoke again. Alone. Then, this time, our gazes locked and... I knew it was somethin' special. I remember running back *instantly* to tell Curtis about it. How I felt about this woman? I'd been without a woman for some time then. I didn't feel I could trust anyone. The details are infractions. He couldn't have been more excited for me. But the feeling I got when I looked into her eyes, it was so... heavenly.

{Mr. Loans listened attentively before responding.}

MR. LOANS: You told her how you feel, and what did she say?

CYRUS: Honestly, I just hope she will feel the same way. Some day.

{Mr. Loans takes a deep breathe before lecturing Cyrus. Pretending he could intercede relevancy.}

MR. LOANS: Cyrus, you feel how you feel, and I'm not taking that away from you.—
{Cyrus abruptly interrupts in a very respectable leveled tone.}

CYRUS: She's the one. I can't eat right. I can't sleep right... without her being on my mind. There's some reason she's come into my life. I have to just know why! I love her and I will do anything... anything to show that. When I'm around her, I just feel like I always want to be the best version of myself. The me I was meant to be.

{*Mr. Loans shakes his head a bit. Cyrus scrolls his head over to Mr. Loans with low peaceful eyes.*}

CYRUS: She kinda reminds me of Mrs. Loans.

MR. LOANS: Hm. Really?

CYRUS: Yeah. The relationship you guys have. Classy and elegant. I remember Mrs. Loans would look out for me and Curtis, and other people before she ever thought about herself when I was a kid. When she would let me tag along with her and Curtis to the supermarket, she was always so polite to everyone. I remember one time... she even paid for some lady's groceries who was next in line. I think the woman was like... counting some change in her hand and Mrs. Loans told the clerk she was paying for the both of them. You know she even drinks as much coffee as Mrs. Loans. Every time I see her, she's got a cup in her hand.

{*Cyrus giggles. Mr. Loans follows suit.*}

MR. LOANS: That's her.

Well son, I can tell you this: if this one isn't the one—and I'm glad you feel the way you do, believe me, I do. If she's not, there will be someone out there special for you. Just you. And you probably won't have to travel back 5 or 6 years to find her love. I don't know what it's like for the new you, but I know "*you*". You deserve the best.

You keep going. Fight for what you love, and never give up. Always have faith in what God has planned for you. Never lose faith in God.

{*Cyrus just smiles widely with his lips clutched. And could do nothing but respect Mr. Loans.*}

CYRUS: Yeah.

Mr. LOANS: So this woman that was murdered was her mother?

{*The rhetorical question. Cyrus gets choked up and his expression changes with a dramatic transition. Thinking back to what happened.*}

CYRUS: ... Yeah.

{*Mr. Loans felt the stress in Cyrus before he even had to look over to see it on him. He changed the subject, and never returned to it the rest of the way home.*}

Not much else is spoken after that. A chuckle or two about fantasy sports, but nothing of importance. They arrive at the Loans household, and head inside as the rain had stopped for a slight moment in time.}

MR. LOANS: Curtis! Dinner's down here!

{*Mrs. Loans comes from the kitchen with a wide smile wearing vibrant red lipstick. Also Dressed in a navy blue and white polka dot dress with skinny jeans underneath. She wore a red headband to hold her hair from her face. Delighted to see Cyrus in one piece.*}

MRS. LOANS: Cyrus! Oh, my boy!

{*She places her hands on Cyrus's shoulders as though he were still 13 years old. Safe to say, she hadn't adjusted to the concept of Cyrus being an adult yet.*}

MRS. LOANS: Are you okay?

CYRUS: Yeah, I'm fine.

{Curtis comes rumbling down the staircase in his socks. You can tell he was wearing socks by the abrasive brushing of his feet on the wooden stairs.

He fronted Cyrus with wide eyes.}

CURTIS: You okay?

{Young Curtis checking on him as he always did annoyed Cyrus since now, he was standing face to face with the 14-year-old version of him.}

CYRUS: Yeah I'm fine, Curtis.

MR. LOANS: Curt' go wash your hands. Dinner will be on the table in a sec.

{Curtis goes rushing back up the stairs.}

Mrs. Loans, Cyrus, and Mr. Loans make their way to the kitchen where there were empty containers seated on the countertop closest to the silver kitchen sink, and next to the sink and counter, the white old wooden back door to the right. There was also an opened box of name-branded cereal on the countertop next to an opened box of fruit snacks.

To the left of the entrance of the kitchen was the large wooden kitchen table. Funny seeing as though this was only a family of three.

Mr. Loans placed the pizza down on the table.}

MR. LOANS: You wanna have a seat, son?

{It may have made Mr. Loans uneasy for Cyrus to be so out of tune observing the kitchen he had been in a million times before. Cyrus walks around to the side of the wooden chair closest to the center of the laminated floor. Slides his bottom on the cold seat facing Mr. Loans who's now seated by the kitchen entrance way closest to the hallway behind him opening the pizza box. Mrs. Loans standing in between the two.}

MRS. LOANS: You... want something to drink, Cyrus?

CYRUS: Uhm, maybe just water. Thank you.

MR. LOANS: Wanna grab some plates too, Hun?

{Mrs. Loans opens the cupboard to grab glasses and dishes. Mr. Loans realized that it was a bit darker at this time of day because of the weather; he reached

back to his left where the light switch was. The room's lighting had a yellowish tone. This light bulb had to have been installed in the late 90s. Mrs. Loans comes to the table with the green plates and clear crystal drinking glasses.}

MR. LOANS: So, what are you gonna do there, Cyrus?

{Cyrus adopts an expression of expectation.}

CYRUS: I'm going to find him.

MRS. LOANS: Why don't we let the police handle this manner?

{Mrs. Loans was irritable. Clearly concerned about Cyrus.}

CYRUS: He can do what I can do. You saw what he did to those police on the news? Somebody's gotta stop him. I really don't think they can. It's gotta be me.

MR. LOANS: You're the only one who knows how those powers work, right?

Who else is gonna do it, Hun? This guy needs his teeth kicked in!
{*Mr. Loans starts chopping down on a slice of pizza before he even had a plate in front of him.*}

MR. LOANS: The question remains, how you gonna find this guy? He's on the move.

CYRUS: The news said he's held up in an abandoned gas station on the outskirts of town.

{*Cyrus responded to the question in an assuming tone.*}

CYRUS: The question is, how will I get past all those cops. My powers are of no help right now.

{*Mrs. Loans growing more irritable as she slams Cyrus's plate in front of him, and then places her right fist on her hip.*}

MRS. LOANS: But you don't actually have powers right now, right? So how are you gonna stop him?

{*Cyrus loved that Mrs. Loans was concerned about him, but also felt smothered. He could only giggle to ward off possible hovering irritation.*}

CYRUS: Mrs. Loans, I know you're worried about me, but I'm the only one who can stop him. It's gotta be me!

{*Mrs. Loans throws her hands in defeat and walks out of the kitchen. You could hear her politely yell for Curtis from the bottom of the stairwell.*}

MRS. LOANS: CURTIS! Come on down, sweetie!

CURTIS: Just a second, Mom!

{*Mrs. Loans doesn't hear much upstairs. Which was always a cause for concern when "with teenagers".*}

MRS. LOANS: Curtis, what are you doing up there?

CURTIS: I was just washing my hands!

{*Curtis comes rumbling down the stairs again.*

Mr. Loans turns the pizza box towards Cyrus as he munches down. Then swiftly rubs a finger or two over the tip of his nose. Men always get this irritation from moving the upper lip of their mouths so much. The more it moved, the more the fizzled hairs above the lip and into the nose itched. No matter how leveled the mustache situation was.}

MR. LOANS: Go ahead and have something to eat.

{Cyrus contently grabs a slice and places it on his plate.

As Mrs. Loans and Curtis head for the kitchen, the home telephone begins to ring from the living room stopping them in the hallway. It rang just three times before Mrs. Loans was able to answer.

She listens...}

MRS. LOANS: ... Oh my, God!

{Mr. Loans, without a second to think, worries from the kitchen. He wipes his mouth with a balled-up paper towel that had been left on the table next to him as he ate. Then he arises.}

MR. LOANS: Elois!? What's going on in there, honey?

ELOIS LOANS: ELVIN! Get in here!

{Elvin Loans rushes to the living room and rhetorically

requests the phone from Elois. He hears the voice of the person, and instantly knew this was trouble.}

ELVIN LOANS: ... What do you want!?

{Cyrus focuses on the sound around the plain white wall blocking the kitchen from the living room. It had a calendar on it near the living room entrance. Dated the year 2006. Another piece out of place in the year 2008.}

ELVIN LOANS: Why are doing this to him!?

{Cyrus's chest began to overheat with adrenaline. He rises up and storms towards the living room. He knew who was on the other end of the phone.

Curtis stood at the living room entrance with that feeling you'd get as an adolescent teen when you came to the revelation that even your parents didn't have the answers to every question life posed. Cyrus hurried over to Loanses.}

CYRUS: Hand me the phone.

{Elvin Loans turned to Cyrus to the right of him. He

hands the phone over. Reporters awaiting the re-sponse of a professional athlete were more silent.}

IGOR: I was beginning to think I would get caught out there! Nothing like a good ol' "cop chase"!

{Igor did not bother with a, "Hello?". He could hear Cyrus request the phone in the background. Knowing when he felt and heard the change in spartan breath-ing patterns of a male past middle-age, and a young male treading past 'Spartiate', Cyrus was attentive.}

IGOR: Here's where you can find me...

NEWS REPORTER: We are receiving word that the names of the deceased and still severely injured officers have been released from the bombing that occurred ... just over... five hours ago. Before the names will be re-leased to the general public, the Northwestern County Police Department requested: we hold off on the reveal until the families of the victims... have been notified. Which could be within the next hour or so. Let me just say first, we offer our deepest, and sincerest apologies and condolences to the effected victims' families.

CYRUS S1C13: THOSE REASONS WHY

IGOR: I'm at an old manufacturing plant. Get a pen and paper so you can write this down.

{Unconventionally, Cyrus showed no extreme distress.}

CYRUS: "Pen and paper."

{Mr. and Mrs. Loans scattered to find a pen and paper. Curtis stood still like he'd watched his favorite Saturday morning cartoon hero rumbling with a super villain like he wished he still could when he was younger, and the hero was losing.}

MRS. LOANS: Curtis go to your room, honey.

{Curtis still watched.

On the phone, a not so awkward pause in conversation as there was no air of remiss between the two. Only the flaunting of dynamic necessary teeth licking from Cyrus. Who probably had cheese, basil and pizza crust deposits in his teeth. And the breathing of Igor.

Mrs. Loans found the 'pen and paper' and hand them over to Cyrus.}

MRS. LOANS: Here.

CYRUS: I got it.

IGOR: ... Just north of that gas station on the news—you've seen the news, right? They had the news helicopters trailing me all the way out. —

CYRUS: Yeah I've seen it.

IGOR: About 5 miles down the road, there's an old manufacturing building. I'll be there. Named, "Henry's Best Auto Parts".

CYRUS: I got it.

IGOR HANNICK: Oh! And be sure to come alone of course!

CYRUS: Yeah, I'll be there! I know!

CLICK!

{Silence.}

MR. LOANS: Where's he at? Let's go get em'.

{Mr. Loans began the dive searching for his car keys.}

CYRUS: Elvin!

*{Elvin stopped in his tracks. Knowing what Cyrus would say next. Cyrus rarely **ever** called him by his first name.}*

CYRUS: I have to go alone.

{Silence.}

MRS. LOANS: Curtis I thought I asked you to go to your room, please! Go!

{This episode had become mundane. The Superheroes were flustered and defeated, and the super villain was no longer around! Besides, "much too old for cartoons now". Curtis turns to the stairwell, and then trots upward. To be continued.}

CYRUS: I can beat this guy.

{Mr. Loans stood there in his old brown faux leather jacket with old coffee stains like he was attending a funeral. Sorrowed and powerless.}

CYRUS: Keys.

{Mr. Loans still didn't know where—oh, in his pocket. He hands them to Cyrus, and Cyrus heads for the door without another word. The door slams, Mrs. Loans jumps.

Silence.

Elvin turns to Elois with sorrowed eyes before embracing his next words with high belief.}

ELVIN: He can do this...

{*The road is clear. The theory is that everyone was terrified of this "IGOR HANNICK" on the loose. That anxiety caused Cyrus to reach for his pocket for his pills again, but remembered rhythmically they weren't there. Cyrus could only think of how every decision he's made has led him to this road. All for the love of Elizabeth Wilson. Was he making a big mistake? What if she still doesn't love him the way he loves her? Was this the only way? Is this his destiny? And what of his father? What would he say? Yes, he'd probably be proud. Cyrus has finally found something meaningful in his life to fight for. Something worthwhile. Not materialistic.*

Cyrus reaches the open highway. What's to the sides of the roads was not relevant. He was tunnel vision-ed on the drive as he attempted to white out all of the secondary thoughts he had to not go after Igor; to turn around. Anxiety, and that continuous thought of Elizabeth Wilson kept him driving. Picking up the speed 2 notches with every second thought. This continued down the road less traveled all the way to where police crowded the road with lights high beaming as the rain had cleared up again showing the sun. Oddly, it was past 7 PM in this late winter night. Another inconsistency in the patterns around him since he arrived in 2008. Cyrus drives past observing the chaos Hannick had created. There were officers directing the few cars that had to pass down the road to the furthest throughway from the gas station where they still believed Igor shacked up. He looked to the officer directing the traffic, then continued on his path.

Another 7 miles, and Cyrus had reached his destination. He was irritable at 5 miles, because Igor quoted the warehouse was 5 miles away from the gas station. This just fired him up more to take this unbelievable rebel down.

The lot of the warehouse was gravel as Cyrus got out of the car without a hesitation. There was no more room to pump fake on his decision to go after Igor. He had to now. The warehouse had steel paneling and a huge sign that read, "Henry's Best Auto Parts". This was the place. It seemed there had been no maintenance past the span of the previous holiday season and the previous fall. Wet, dirt-brown leaves blew across the grounds. Cyrus walked up to the steel front door that had a white light just above it. The sun had gone down within the span of thirty minutes. Cyrus opened the door and walked in. He slowly paced towards the center of the room where the lighting resided. Before then, there was nothing but the rummaging of someone on the opposite side of the center stage. Igor sat with his back facing the center of the floor before turning around as Cyrus appeared like the main attraction of a theater performance. Igor seemed to be working on something. There was an orb on the crafting table glowing so vividly. The old, scrapped auto parts to the side of the orb were overlooked.}

IGOR HANNICK: You're here!

{*Cyrus was calm and quiet. These were generally the most dangerous people in society, because their silence meant they were prepared for war. There was nothing more to talk about. The current world according to Cyrus O'Brian.*}

IGOR HANNICK: You know, I was thinking about down at the police station... —

{*Cyrus snapped with a scream that was yet a snaring mutter.*}

CYRUS: YOU SON OF A MOTHERFUCKING BITCH! I SWEAR TO **GOD** I'M GOING TO KILL YOU!

{*Igor snapped.*}

IGOR HANNICK: Oh, NO, NO, NO! HE'S NOT HERE TO PROTECT YOU THIS TIME, YOU WHINEY PIECE OF SHIT!

{*This felt amiss to Cyrus. **Who** was protecting him? He'd just met Igor!*}

Igor began a muttering spat.}

IGOR HANNICK: All these years! *You* were his favorite! He kept *you*, and protected *you*. Better than he did the rest of us! You have the nerve to step in front of me?... like this!?

{Igor let out a cry for help in the form of a snicker that didn't seem to have the confidence Igor had had all this time. Cyrus needed Igor to stay relevant on the topic at hand.}

CYRUS: You... killed an innocent woman! Then those innocent police officers.

{Tears began to fall from Igor's eyes. Amiss was replaced by emotionally relatability of extreme esteem and combustion as Cyrus saw distress in Igor.}

IGOR HANNICK: I've killed... and killed... and killed!

{Igor attempted to wipe his tears and bottle his emotions, but he had clearly been broken. Igor seemed to have become the victim. How dare this murderous psychopath act as though he'd been the one affected the most by his own actions? Was this remorse? Or regret?—No! He said before he felt no guilt.}

IGOR: I've... *killed* and *killed*!

{*Igor takes swift twirls putting his hands on his head.*}

IGOR: I've killed and killed.

{*He began to whisper to himself. Repeating the same things.*

Cyrus squints completely lost for words. His anger seemed misdirected now.}

CYRUS: Sonya Wilson was her name!

{*Cyrus did not want the subject to change. He needed Igor to* **stay on topic***! This was his moment of pain.* **He** *was supposed to be angry.* **Not** *Igor. He didn't even* **know** *Igor! Why should he feel pity for his tears when he'd murdered the mother of the woman he loves?*}

IGOR: I...

{*Igor continued to be discombobulated.*}

IGOR: This is all your fault... This is just... all your fault!

{Cyrus was over this more than obvious miscommunication.}

CYRUS: What is my *"fault"*!?

{Igor grabs a gun from underneath the table where the orb sat. As he rose, he had a smile on his face as vivid as photogenic could have, but tears disrupted the appeal of this vigilant portrait. He pointed the gun at Cyrus. Cyrus took a step backwards before he un-miraculously stood his ground.}

CYRUS: Dude I don't even know you!

{Hannick wore that smile again as he did that day he drove a knife through the gut of Sonya Deanne Wilson.}

IGOR: BUT WE ALL KNOW YOU! We all... know... you!

CYRUS: Who is *"we"*!? Man, what the—... are you even *talking* about!?

IGOR: I've gone through multiple times—many dimensions and universes. Looking to find you. All of us! There are more of us! Spread across different time loops. We've been pitted against each other like animals in a cathedral—colosseum. Survival of the fittest. The more you kill, the more power you get.

{Cyrus was now simply listening.}

IGOR: But killing you... *you* were off limits. God has been protecting his most "prestigious" asset. Like you were better than the rest of us. WHAT ABOUT US! Huh!?

{More tears from Hannick as he pretended to not be the man he accused the man across from him of being. He put his free hand back on his head and bent over. He was unequivocally out of control of himself. Cyrus's anger was now obsolete.}

IGOR: What about *us*? The—... She... my love...

{Igor peered up from his broken bent stance.}

IGOR: They killed her. All the people I loved. Dead. All for "*power*"! Was it worth it? You think "*power*" is worth it? Because... now it is to me! Well, this time, I

TAKE CONTROL! ME! ME! MEEEEEE!

{Igor pointed the gun.}

IGOR: I... WANT POWER, CYRUS!

{Cyrus felt compassion now hearing Igor's testimony. Even though he didn't know the entire story, he knew it to be a true one. He'd never witnessed anyone with such pain in their spirit. Completely at the mercy of his own life.

Even as defenseless as Cyrus was now, he was armored completely for what would come next, because he had the upper hand emotionally.}

CYRUS: Hey, whatever it is, man... —

IGOR HANNICK: JUST SHUT UP! Just... shut up, you punk! I just need you to die! —

CYRUS: ("Punk?" Who still... —) WAIT, wait, wait, wait, wait! Wait... wait! What's the orb? What's the orb for?

{Igor knew Cyrus was stalling, but Cyrus needed to

know his pain. Cyrus looked past Igor to the glowing orb now vividly radiating like a star. Igor too peered over to it for a second.}

IGOR: It's my energy source! The reason your powers aren't workin'... is because once two of us are in the same time loop, our powers dissipate. I store my power in this orb to use when I travel. This is how I am able to use my powers while you're here.

{As Igor spoke, Cyrus was attempting to come up with a plan, but he had nothing.}

POW!

{Igor fires a bullet.}

[Back at the Loans Household.]

RING, RING, RING!

MR. LOANS: Hello?

PHONE CALLER: Hi, it's Theresa, is Cyrus there?

MRS. LOANS: Who is it, Elvin?

{*Elvin evaded Eloise's question to not worry her any more than she already was by giving her a direct answer that would spark an on-going conversation while he was already occupied with the phone call at hand.*}

MR. LOANS: Hey, Theresa. How are you?

THERESA: I'm fine.

This Elvin? Got the word Cyrus was posted bail by this guy around the city blowing things up. This doesn't look good even though we got a confession from this "*Igor Hannick*" fellow. This could be portrayed as some kind of convoluted partnership. Where is Cyrus now?

ELVIN: He's... not here right now.

THERESA: ... Elvin, what the hell is going on? Where is he!?

ELVIN: He... went out to grab a bite to eat. —

THERESA: Oh, God. Elvin don't do this! Where is he!?

{*Elvin faulted his response with insecurity.*}

THERESA: I've known you too long, Elvin. Don't do this to me. Now I took this case out of love and respect for the family. Respect I have for you and Elois! —

ELVIN: I know, I know —

THERESA: Now you're doing this to me behind my back? —

ELVIN: No—I know, I get it—

THERESA: No, Elvin. I put myself on the line for this case. With little-to-nothing to go on.

ELVIN: I know, I know. I'm sorry. I... we can't really tell you, Theresa. He's... gone after this guy.

THERESA: What? What do you—what does that mean? The *entire* city is at a loss for this entire situation. I'm no PR rep. I'm not here to make this all look good, and that's not what I can do. I can't actually make that happen. I can only do what I *can* to make sure Cyrus gets the best of this situation, and I cannot do that if you are treating me like the reporters who are covering this case!

ELVIN: Theresa, there's—is much more to this than we know ourselves. Now you'll just have to believe me when I say—

THERESA: I've *been* believing you, Elvin! When are you going to show me why I believed in you to begin with!?—

ELVIN: I fucking can't with this—talk to your friend!

{*Elvin murmurs to himself as he hands the phone over to Elois.*}

THERESA: ELOIS! What the fuck is going on here!?— I'm sorry, "What the hell is going on here!?"

{*Elvin continued to murmur to himself as he exits.*}

ELVIN: Unbelievable Theresa thinks we're still in college the way she talks.

ELOIS: Theresa, there isn't much we can do right now...

[Back at Henry's Best Auto Parts.]

{*Cyrus laid on his back motionless on the concrete floor. A bullet to the chest. Eyes closed.*

In the darkness he laid. Silence up close. In the absolute far distance he could still hear reality. Until a white light shined and brightened as it moved closer to him. He was sure he had died. A vibrational volume of a magnitude no human could withstand rang as the light approached Cyrus. Through the vibration, a harmonious sound also of great magnitude awoke Cyrus like this had all been a dream. But only in this realm. In the realm where he'd been shot, the bullet that pierced his chest removed itself from his chest in the same pattern it had struck him in.}

IGOR: What the... you gotta be fucking kidding me!

{*Igor prepared to point his gun again.*}

IGOR: Of course!

{*Cyrus's eyes opened, and he rose. That same bullet*

that struck him, hung in the air, and then dropped to the ground. So Igor clutched the handle of the gun to fire another.}

CYRUS: **PAUSE!**

TIME & IGOR'S BODY PAUSES!

IGOR: (What the—... how the... I can't fucking move!)

*{He walked towards Igor like a fable out of a prophecy. Igor looked back over his right shoulder with his eyeballs, as far as he could see, in the direction of his orb. He could not **see** it, because he could **not** move his neck! He was conscious of it all. The orb unraveled a potent attacking light that allowed Igor to gain his mobility again. By the time he tried to fire his gun at Cyrus, Cyrus was within arm's reach and grabbed ahold of the gun. The two wrestled with the gun crashing into the table where the orb sat. The orb wobbled and wobbled as they wrestled. Grunting and fighting for their lives, the orb fell from the table onto the floor... and broke. Unleashing a light brighter than light itself. And the only thing that could be seen... was white.}*

CYRUS S1C14: BORN THE YEAR 19' SOMETHING / LIZ'S REALITY

{*Darkness, again, is all Cyrus could see. What had happened? It was like the second trimester of pregnancy for the baby itself, Cyrus could remember the shrouding darkness and unrecognizable voices from outside of the black he was coveted in in the belly of his mother. He slowly attempted to open his eyes for the first time. Where and when was he? The voices he heard began to clear as his vision did.*}

VOICES: What read do we have on him now?

VOICES: Still unresponsive.

VOICES: And he was just found in a coma like this?

VOICES: Yes. Signs are showing it's a direct correlation— we found heavy amounts of... various opioids in his system.

VOICES: Hm. Yeah I had time to read his board. How could someone get all of those opioids in their system at once? He's stable though, correct?

VOICES: ... Yes, we have him sedated and all of his vitals are leveled and balanced.

CYRUS: (What the hell is going on? Wha'... where... what's going on!? I can't move! God I can't move! Someone!...)

{Cyrus's vision began to clear up as he saw a doctor with dark brown short hair approaching him with a stethoscope around his neck.}

DOCTOR: His eyes are open now.

{Cyrus could also see the female down towards the end of what was clearly a hospital bed he was in over the edge of his feet covered by a baby blue cotton quilted blanket. She wore a pink scrub. The complete set including the nurse's cap.}

DOCTOR: Get a read for me really quick?

{The nurse rushes over to the right bed side of Cyrus out of his sight.}

NURSE: Oxygen and heart rate increasing.

{The Doctor had a clipboard that he picked up from nowhere and began to write like a child on a field trip to a history or science museum.}

DOCTOR: Okay.

He's got... tears. Wonder if he knows what happened. Let's manage his vitals, and if he completely comes out, let's just issue him on rehabilitation release.

{Those were the last words Cyrus heard as his breathing became heavy, and his picture shaded slowly like a video editor moving the exposure meter of the cinema towards negative levels. A small task for film editing after the year... let's say, 2010.}

{Cyrus awoke again, but maybe he'd already been awake. He was able to move his body now. Sluggishly, as if he'd been released from the womb now, and held by a doctor for the first time. He was seated in what felt to be a thinly seated wheelchair. He was moving, but his feet were not on the waxed tile floors. Very uncomfortable. He was being rolled down a half white, half green hallway with "EXIT" signs, and more doctors around him. He felt crowded even though some of the doctors were drifting by momentarily.

He was then brought to an empty room with a thin mattress and dresser next to it. He was scrolled to the center of the room where he looked down to see he had been restrained by the arms and feet. He was also wearing scrubs. Then, he heard more speaking as the person who had scrolled him into this room had left him to himself.}

VOICES: What's this guy's story?

{This was a man.}

VOICE #2: Someone checked him in. Says they knew him. I don't know. The hospital said he had enough opioids in his system to kill an elephant. He's been heavily sedated. They suggested we strap him in as well. We received his file, and he has numerous cases of psychiatric meltdowns.

{Another man.

Cyrus was still barely mobile hearing the two men talking from behind him in the near distance.}

MALE VOICE #1: Damn. Well, they know how long he's gonna be here?

MALE VOICE #2: No word. I'm figuring a while though

with his history.

CYRUS: (What "psychiatric meltdowns"? I don't even have—I do regularly doctor checkups! What "history"? I haven't done pills in a *week*... How!? Who put me here!? Where am I!? Where's Igor, *you* motherfuckerssss!... Elizabeth!... What happened!?)

{*In his scrambled thoughts, he made out an unbelievable fact from the voices...*}

MALE VOICE #2: He's got meltdowns from 1957.

MALE VOICE #1: Damn. So this guy has been bonkers for around 10 years!

CYRUS: (... You gotta be fucking kidding me.)

[Back in the Year 2008.]

{*The police eventually raided the gas station and found out Igor was* **nowhere** *to be found. They eventually made their way down to Henry's Best Auto Parts where they found an unused and old vacant building. They searched and searched the city and issued warrants for the whereabouts and arrest of Igor Hannick,*} *but nothing came of it. The same for Cyrus who was still technically only out on bond until his trial. A month passed, and eventually, the masses began to forget about the odd and notorious story of the 'Time Traveler & The Terrorist' as they did with every story before it.}*

[At the Wilson household.]

{Steve sat on the couch in front of the fireplace like he always did with Elizabeth. But this time, and for the months prior, he sat in the living room with all of the windows closed, the lights down, and alone. Glaring at the cold fireplace across from him. Elizabeth stood midway on the stairs and studied him multiple times. Often also at the front door. Even though she knew her mother wasn't coming back home to her and her father.}

RING, RING, RING!

{The telephone rang constantly before Steve decided it was in his best interest to answer it.}

STEVE: Hello, this is 'Steven Wilson'.

{On the other side of the line, there was a cold silence for 2 to 3 seconds. Steven was preparing to repeat his introduction, but the person spoke.}
PHONE CALLER: ... Hi... my name is 'Elvin Loans'.

STEVEN: Okay, how can I help you Mr. Loans? I'm really not in the mood for cold calls, sorry.

{*Steven assumed Elvin was an unexperienced salesman and was already ready to get off of the line with him.*}

ELVIN LOANS: No, I'm not selling anything. Sorry to bother you, I just wanted to reach out to you, and tell you how sorry I am for your loss.—I... am a friend of Cyrus, and I wanted to reach out to ya' myself.

{*This was a heart racing moment. Steven sat up on his couch from his slouched position to attend more care to the phone call. He was... speechless.*}

ELVIN LOANS: I wanted to meet with you in person and talk to you personally. Can we meet?

{*Steve was vacant of mind, and blindly agreed.*}

STEVE: Uhm, yeah. When?

[Later that evening at Frappes Cafe.]

{*Elvin arrived early to the cafe wearing his coffee-stained brown jacket. He sat at the table fiddling with his cup of steaming hot coffee as Steven Wilson walked through the front entrance and caught sight of him. Steve met Elvin's eyes and knew that was the man he was looking for. He walked over wearing an old, peeled leather coat, and took a seat across from Elvin.*}

ELVIN: ... Nice coat.

STEVEN: Thanks, my uhh... Sonya bought it for me for our second anniversary.

{*Speaking as though Elvin personally knew Sonya Deanne. Maybe because he felt his privacy had already been invaded over the last few months.*}

ELVIN: Got some nice weather out there. Almost too warm for our nice jackets and coats now, haha.

STEVEN: Yeah, yeah, ahaha...

So...

ELVIN: Yes.

Nice to meet ya', first and foremost... I just wanted to say again... how sorry I am. I know it's been rough on you and your family for the last few months. Last person you're expecting to hear from is —... How ya' doin'?

STEVEN: As best as I can. Thank you.

{Steve showed a lack of patience he attempted to subdue. Yet he was also empathetic of the fact that he didn't understand much of anything. Best to sit and listen while his mind, spirit and body find some kind of balance.}

ELVIN: So, I just wanted to reach out. I know it's hard and... I wanted... you to hear some of Cyrus's side of the story. I know you may be hurt by all this, and some of the blame could go to Cyrus, because he was there. But I just wanted to reassure you... that *Cyrus O'Brian* is a *great* kid, and he was just there to help. Believe me. He may have these moments and days, but... his heart was in the right place. It always is.

{Elvin grinned to assure Steve that he was sincere. Steve still had his doubts.}

STEVEN: They haven't been able to find Cyrus for some time either.

ELVIN: Cyrus... after all that happened, he had to leave town.

STEVEN: But he was only released on bond. —

ELVIN: I know, I know, but...

{*Elvin still attempting to assure Steven of why Cyrus should not be considered the antagonist in his story. Still rambling through this **seemingly** unrehearsed 'sales pitch'. Elvin knew that he had no idea of what happened to Cyrus either that night, but he **needed** to convince Steve. All he knew was that he **believed** in Cyrus. While Steve was inwardly pleading with himself to be forgiving and understanding.*}

ELVIN: He didn't do it. I'm tellin' ya'.

{*Elvin held back the next statement that would have sent him down the **shit** hole of bad sales rapport building; telling a man he knew his pain, when he had no idea what he felt exactly. Trying to wrench out a truth based on your own sales merit is like considering your life to be more important. As though you had no time to listen to others. Allow the person to open up and unveil their pain themselves.*}

STEVEN: Yeah.

{Steve was fighting back tears now.}

STEVEN: She wasn't happy.

{Elvin listened compassionately to what could follow this vague statement. Bingo.}

STEVEN: She was surrounding herself with... people—women who were not caring of her. They all looked out for themselves. But my wife, Sonya, she's from New York City. She always wore this... strong face. That's why I loved her so much. You know, I'm all... sensitive... and she... was always the strong one for me. She always had an answer. Ahaha. Guess that's why those other women didn't care for her too much.

{Elvin continued to listen silently without breaking eye contact.}

STEVEN: She was overwhelmed. So I was going to have my Nanny's family move into our guest house to help take care of household chores and to do things like pick up Liz'—Elizabeth from school, because Nanny couldn't drive, ahaha. It was okay. I met her cousins a couple Christmases ago, and they were all good to us.

The best people I'd ever met. So I figured, "why not?".

Sonya was going to spend time back home in New York. With all her family. Her father's sick still. Her mother needed help taking care of him. And she wanted to be around all of her cousins and relatives—huge family. And no matter how much she loved us...

{*Steven had now surpassed his pain threshold. He began to crumble.*}

STEVEN: I had a feeling she would have never come back to us. Now that Sonya's gone. For good... I'm going to still need their help even more now.

{*Tears now flowing uncontrollably. While he still remained composed enough to conduct conversation. Careful not to break. Elvin could do nothing but admire Steve's heart and the love he possessed. And his willingness to continue to fight.*}

THE END.

Want More 'CYRUS'?

Visit 'Jacob Hollingsworth Network'
for the latest news & updates.

JACOBHOLLINGSWORTH.NET